VICIOUS CONSEQUENCES

A CONSEQUENCES NOVEL
BOOK 4

AMANDA SIEGRIST

Cover Designer: Amanda Siegrist
Photos provided by: idal/VitalikRadko/Depositphotos.com
Edited by: Editing Done Write

Also By Amanda Siegrist

A happy ending is all I need.

Consequences Novel

Dark Consequences

Cruel Consequences

Fatal Consequences

Vicious Consequences

Haunting Love Novel

Third Time's the Charm

Thirteen Days Gone

One Mistake Too Late

Holiday Romance Novel

Merry Me

Mistletoe Magic

Christmas Wish

Snowed in Love

Snowflakes and Shots

Holiday Hope

Sleigh All the Way

Lucky Town Novel

Escaping Memories

Dangerous Memories

Stolen Memories

Deadly Memories

Forgotten Memories

McCord Family Novel

Protecting You

Trust in Love

Deserving You

Always Kind of Love

Finding You

Dare You to Love

Mona & Mason

The Paranormal Chronicles, Volume 1

Perfect For You Novel

The Wrong Brother

The Right Time

The Easy Part

The Hard Choice

Psychic Love Novel

Exploding Love

Captured Love

Slaying Love Novel

Won't Let You Go

Doomed Love

Deadly Crazy

Evidence of Sin

Finding Redemption

Obsessed Hope

Short Stories

Paint By Murder

Follow Me, Sweet Darling

Sleighville Novel

Dashing Through the Fear

Here Comes Chaos

The Last Noel

Standalone Novel

The Danger with Love

Conquering Fear Novel

Co-written with Jane Blythe

Drowning in You

Out of the Darkness

Closing In

1

"THIS IS JAKE ANDERS. Don't bother leaving a message because the likelihood I call you back is slim to none."

Beeeeeeeep.

"So what I'm hearing is there's a chance. The actual definition of slim is very small, meaning it is possible." She paused after saying the same thing every time she got his voicemail.

In the past month, it was every single time.

"If you don't want people to think there is a *slim* chance, you should change your voicemail. And what you have now is rude and uncalled for."

Ugh.

She was letting her irritation and anger shine through.

"I would like to retract that last sentence. Please strike it from the record. It is your choice how you manage your voicemail."

She held in a short laugh, but felt better adding a bit of humor only he would understand. A little inside joke between the two of them. He'd dated a lawyer one time. It lasted all of two months, and she had way too much fun teasing him about it, especially when everyone warned him not to date a lawyer.

"Did you know that beavers are the second-largest living rodents, after the capybaras, and they can weigh up to one hundred and ten pounds?"

Commence awkwardness by throwing out a random fact —her specialty.

"Well, let's chat later. Call me."

She ended the message and set her phone on the counter.

"What the hell is a capybaras?"

Jo turned around from the island counter to see her roommate, Ivy.

Ivy waved her hand frivolously in the air, shaking her head. "I take it back. I don't want to know. You'll give me a full history of the dumb animal, and I don't care."

At least she didn't think she'd made up the animal. Because some people thought half the things she said were fabricated. Why would she lie? It made no sense.

"How is Detective Anders?"

Jo frowned.

"Oh, he didn't answer. Again. Why do you keep trying with that man?"

"Rome wasn't built in a day."

Ivy rolled her eyes. "I bet if I asked you, you'd know the exact number of days it took to build."

"Actually—"

"Nope. I don't care." Ivy wrapped an arm around her, squeezing. "But I care about you. Stop calling him. Stop doing this to yourself."

"He's grieving. I won't stop being there for someone in a time of need."

"Jo, you're grieving too."

Yes, well, everyone grieved in different ways. She poured herself into her work, and Jake did the exact opposite. He removed himself from the world. From life itself.

Ivy kissed her on the cheek, then rounded the counter. "Don't wait up for me tonight. I have a hot date."

"Okay." She giggled because she never waited up for her roommate. Because she always had a hot date.

"You know what you need," Ivy said, pointing a finger at her with the milk jug in her other hand. "You need to get laid. It would relax you and de-stress you." She bobbed her head up and down. "And we both know it's been way too long."

Whereas her friend got laid too much. She wouldn't call Ivy loose—ever—but she wasn't cautious with who she gave herself to. Jo was much more cautious.

So much more.

Maybe too cautious.

But she'd never done well with dating. Or men. Or flirting. She was hopeless. They both knew it.

"I know a guy—"

"Did you know that speed dating was invented by Rabbi Yaacov Deyo in the 1990s. He wanted to make it easier for single Jewish people in Los Angeles to meet each other."

"Fine. I hear you. You don't want me to set you up with this cute guy I work with." Ivy drank her glass of milk, a wicked smile on her face after finishing it. "I could find a speed dating night for us. I would totally do it with you. If that's what you're trying to tell me."

Well, that random fact blew up in her face.

"On that note," Jo said, standing up, "I have to get to work. You have fun on your date and don't do anything I wouldn't do."

Ivy hollered at her back. "That's everything. You're Mrs. I-hate-fun!"

Jo shut the door, breathing out a long breath. She loved her roommate to pieces, but she could be a handful at times. Honestly, Ivy was one of the rare few who could put up with her odd tendencies and weird behavior.

She couldn't help herself. When she got nervous or uncomfortable, she spouted facts. All kinds of facts. Random ones. Useless ones. Interesting ones. Most people found her odd, which created problems making friends. When she moved to New York two years ago, she'd moved in with a complete stranger—Ivy—to save money on rent. It had been touch and go at first, but they'd looked past each other's faults—because they both had them—and became more than roommates. They were friends. Jo hated admitting it, but Ivy was about the only friend she had in New York. Her co-workers didn't count. She might go out for a drink or two with them on occasion, but they didn't ask her to join them often. Even at work, she was the odd one out.

But she was used to it. All her life she'd been the oddball, the weird one. It was nothing new and she couldn't change who she was. Nor did she want to. If people couldn't like her for her, they weren't worth her time. Something her brother had told her all the time.

She shook loose any thoughts of her brother and headed for work.

The precinct was bustling with activity when she arrived. As usual. She waved and smiled on her way to her desk, though she received grunts and half-hearted grins in return.

No big deal.

Just because people couldn't return a kindness when receiving one didn't mean she would stop doing it herself.

She worked hard on putting herself out there more. On making the first move, making the first greeting. It wasn't easy. Some days she wanted to glower and glare as much as the rest of them.

Especially in the last two months.

But if she didn't maintain a sunny disposition, she'd fall down the same rabbit hole Jake had fallen in. Then who would save them? She was here to pull him out. To save them both. Sort of. It was kind of difficult to be there for him when she lived in New York and he resided in Minnesota.

"Yo, Jo. Hit me with a fact."

She looked up from her desk to Sterling, one of the detectives in her division—violent crimes—staring at her with anticipation from across the room. Sometimes, people would request this of her—a random fact. It didn't always happen and she hadn't quite figured out if they were making fun of her or not. Or if they enjoyed the weird things she knew.

"Hippopotomonstrosesquippedaliophobia is the fear of long words." Then she returned her focus to the case files on her desk.

She heard snickers from across the room.

That was why she could never figure out if they were teasing her or not. The laughter that always accompanied after she word-vomited facts without hesitating. Why not spread her knowledge? One of these days, they would appreciate her wide variety of information.

"Damn. I'm impressed."

Jo looked up to see Detective Tate Powell standing next to her desk.

"You even pronounced that long ass word without jumbling it up once."

Well, she'd never admit it, but she had practiced saying

it when she came across it. When one spouts facts all the time, one needs to say it clearly and without incident.

"What's the fear of working with idiots?" Tate drawled.

Jo chuckled. Most people didn't like Tate, considering him too brash and insensitive. Maybe she liked him because he didn't pull any punches. He didn't tell lies or pretend to be someone he wasn't. She found him refreshing, when everyone else seemed to hide who they were.

And most importantly, he didn't keep his distance from her. He didn't think she was odd.

"I'm afraid there is no actual phobia of that."

"That's too bad because if I had a phobia, it would be that. I'm surrounded by them." He flashed her a genuine smile. "Have a great day, Jo."

Then he was walking away and she didn't have time to thank him for lifting her spirits.

Because, yes. She was going to have a great day.

THE DOOR SWOOSHED BEHIND THEM, then slammed with a clang. It made him jump, glancing behind him.

Then he was jolted from the sharp voice next to him.

"You're a man-child."

"Seriously?"

"An absolute man-child."

Jason's sister, Junelle, stormed off down the sidewalk, and he was forced to rush after her. "Can you slow down please?"

Junelle stopped and turned toward him. Her disapproval was easy to read. Pinched brows, pressed lips, arms crossed. "You can find your own way home."

"Don't I get a chance to explain?"

"I don't want to hear why you got arrested. It shouldn't have happened in the first place. Grow up, Jason! I won't bail you out next time."

Her pace resumed. He had to walk at a clipped pace to keep up with her. Which was crazy because she had shorter legs than he did. He didn't like the speed at which she walked. It made it harder for him to watch his surroundings. To make sure no one jumped out at him again. He struggled maintaining her momentum while also keeping his eyes peeled at every corner and person they passed.

"I was defending a woman's honor, thank you very much."

"Don't care."

"The guy was—"

Junelle stopped in her tracks. "Violence isn't the answer. You can defend a woman's honor without using your fists. One of these times—maybe it'll be this time—the charges are going to stick. You could find yourself sitting in prison. Is that what you want?"

Of course not. It had to be a rhetorical question.

She released a heavy sigh, her disappointment hitting him in the face like a rough slap. "I love you, Jason. I love that you stick up for women who need it. More men need to do so. But I hate that you put yourself in these kinds of positions. I asked Officer Benson what happened and he said the guy had a knife. A knife." Her words choked at the end.

Jason couldn't handle the torture in her eyes and tore his gaze away to the pavement. The guy had produced a knife. He understood the agony in that simple sentence. Too much.

After Jason shoved the guy when he had grabbed the woman's arm, the dude swung at him. Of course, Jason swung back, hitting him square in the face and knocking him on his ass. When the guy got up from the ground, a pocketknife appeared out of nowhere. Jason hated admitting he froze. If the woman's boyfriend hadn't returned from the restroom at that exact time, the guy would've stabbed him. Would've brought him down without an inch of resistance. But the boyfriend had and stepped in, relieving the dude of the knife. Somehow, all three of them had been arrested for fighting when it should've been the original asshole who started it all by putting his hands on a woman he had no right to.

"I can't do this with you right now. Go home."

He didn't look up for several seconds, and by the time he did, his sister had disappeared around the corner.

She was right. Violence wasn't the answer. He had gotten lucky.

He rubbed his left side, trying to erase the nightmares from so long ago. Yet he relived them so often, it felt like it had happened yesterday.

Seeing the flash of the knife...

The evil in the guy's eyes...

He jumped, darting his gaze every which way. The sidewalk was empty except for him. A brick wall next to him. He was safe. No one could attack him.

He could've been injured last night and it would've been his own fault. It was one thing to help a woman in need. It was another whole thing to freeze up in the middle of the attack.

Jason made his way home and took a shower as soon as he walked through the door. Who knew what kind of disgusting germs were crawling all over him. A cell wasn't the cleanest of places, and it wasn't exactly the Ritz either, so it was no surprise he'd had a rough night of sleeping to boot.

Despite feeling dead on his feet, he resisted the urge to crawl into bed and instead grabbed a bite to eat. By the time he'd had enough to get him through the next few hours, he called his foreman, Terry. They chatted for a bit, with Terry giving him updates, and then ended the call.

Jason never worried when he wasn't around because Terry handled everything with ease. In the past year since he'd been injured, Terry had to step up to the plate with his construction business. There were some days he struggled even getting out of bed. Lack of sleep producing headaches that incapacitated him. Of course, he never told his sister about them, or his parents. He didn't want everyone worrying about him.

He'd get a handle on everything soon. He had to. Letting the asshole win would never happen. He'd fought death, and he'd fight this battle too.

There was no reason for him to go in today. He had a bunch of paperwork to catch up on. While he loved getting his hands dirty and working with his crew, he didn't have to as the owner of the company. That's what Terry was for.

He opened his computer and got down to work. The day dragged on, his mind wandering more than it should've. And not about what happened last night at the bar either. He should've never gone out in the first place, but a buddy of his had dragged him out, and then shit happened. He wasn't going to dwell on it.

No, his mind kept wandering back to the day over a year ago, walking with his sister and then feeling the searing pain in his side. Then nothing but darkness. For weeks. He'd been stabbed five times, nearly died, was in the ICU in a coma for weeks, and no matter how hard he tried, he couldn't stop his brain from reliving it. At the most inopportune times too.

By the time five o'clock rolled around, his brain was fried from trying to concentrate and failing. He needed to get out of his apartment. Maybe being on site would help. He should've gone into work today to get his mind off things best forgotten.

He packed up his laptop and left for work. They had their moveable offices set up at the current construction site they were working on. Renovating an old office building into apartments. It was a big contract they landed, and he needed everything to go smoothly. The client was difficult on occasion, changing things at the last minute. Or wanting him to order supplies from companies he'd never used before. He understood about cutting costs when applicable, but it wasn't always the safest bet.

When he got to the site, the place was deserted. No surprise there. Everyone clocked out at five. He was a firm believer that work was not everything. He didn't expect his employees to work overtime, unless absolutely necessary. His company paid well, had good benefits, ample vacation time, and he treated them with respect. It helped him have a low turnover rate and more loyal employees. Not even Terry was in the office when he stepped inside.

Of course, his mind wandered again, even in the office, so he gave up trying to work on his computer. He'd been holed up in the office the past week trying to catch up on paperwork. Maybe it was time he took a break and used manual labor to clear his mind.

He packed up his laptop and locked it in his truck, then decided he'd take a look around the building, see the progress they were making. Deciding to start at the top and work his way down, he climbed the stairs to the tenth floor. This wasn't one of the larger buildings in the neighborhood. He appreciated that sentiment as his legs got a workout.

Sure, he could've taken the elevator, but that would've defeated the purpose of what he was trying to do—clear his mind with strenuous activity. He wasn't going to do any physical labor tonight. It wasn't wise to do that alone and with no one knowing he was here, not smart at all. But the jaunt up the flight of stairs and walking around the building would help him somewhat. He'd done this a few times and it helped.

When he reached the eighth floor, he paused.

What was that sound?

No one should be here.

He wasn't exactly sure what he heard, but he knew he shouldn't have heard anything.

Flinging open the stairwell door, he stepped into the hallway. Equipment lined both sides of the walls. He had to walk carefully, stepping around stuff.

His feet froze when he heard another sound. Muffled crying?

"Hello?"

A low cry rented the air followed by a scream. Then a shadow darted out a doorway at the end of the hallway. Jason made a mad dash for the individual.

Because whoever they were, he knew they weren't one of his employees.

Footsteps rattled and echoed down the stairwell as he gave chase. By the time he made it back down to the main level, he was nearly out of breath, and whoever had fled was out of his sight.

Damn it!

Jason made his way back up the stairs to see what the person had been doing. He froze in the doorway of the room the person had fled.

In the corner of what would be a living room when it

was completed lay a woman, huddled in the corner, crying. Her clothes were torn and she had marks all over her body.

It didn't take a genius to figure out what had happened.

"Shit. You're okay now. I'm calling the police."

He pulled his phone out, his fingers hovering over the screen, when another voice from behind him made him shiver.

"Hands up where I can see them. You're under arrest."

Holy hell.

His sister was going to kill him. And this time, it wasn't even his fault.

2

Nooooo!

Why had that stupid man been there? He hadn't been finished. He'd barely even started.

The woman had come with him willingly. They always did. They could never resist his charm.

He'd perfected at a young age how to get what he wanted. It didn't take much to flash an alluring grin and get women to fall under his spell. It didn't hurt he had a handsome face to go with his smooth words. He knew that. It wasn't conceit talking or anything. It was fact.

Sometimes, he flirted, he wooed, he wined and dined them. Even took a few of them on dates before getting what he wanted. Their complete and total submission. Those women were the lucky ones. The ones who saw the nice side of him. The ones who didn't have to worry about anything but how good he made them feel. He let them walk away to live the rest of their life.

Then there were times his not-so-nice side came out. It didn't happen often. He worked hard at keeping that side hidden. Letting out the evil side led to trouble. It was a side effect to his life that was...unavoidable. And if the women who were unlucky enough to witness that side listened and followed his directions, he would never have to hurt them.

So really, it was their fault. Not his. If they obeyed him like good little girls, he would never have to hurt them. To use force. They could enjoy what he was offering them.

Pleasure like they'd never had before.

The woman he just left didn't get to experience his full pleasure. She didn't get to know how special she was.

All because of that stupid man, whoever he was.

It was a good thing he kept in shape. Getting away had been a breeze. He didn't break a sweat running down the flight of stairs and out on the street.

No one even looked at him funny as he ran. New York. So many weirdos nobody even paid attention anymore.

He doubled back to the construction site. He needed to know who had surprised him. Because he'd cased the joint for over two weeks, knowing it'd be empty. He'd planned it all down to the very last detail.

Except when he turned down the street, it was flashing with red and blue lights.

Damn!

The police had already arrived. That was fast.

How could they have been so fast?

He kept walking down the street, gawking as much as the other people gathering on the street, but not enough to draw attention. He needed to blend in.

Stopping wouldn't be safe, so he kept walking until he reached the corner and turned.

He'd made an error today. A colossal one.

The woman was still alive.

She hadn't gotten the full pleasure she deserved, nor had he.

Nothing but a loose end.

And if there was one thing he never did was leave loose ends.

All she wanted to do was go home and take a long, hot bath. She loved taking baths to de-stress. Working in the violent crimes unit meant she took a lot of baths. They served two purposes. One, to relax her body and mind from the day. Two, cleanse herself of the violence she dealt with every single day.

She never dealt with the pretty stuff. Not that any crime was pretty. But she handled all the ugly, disgusting things people did to one another.

Like rape.

She hated that particular crime the most.

So when she heard the call over the radio, especially being close to the location, she drove there instead of home. Then to get the suspect right away. Even better.

She'd slapped handcuffs on him, grateful when backup arrived shortly after her. They removed him from the room, and she went to comfort the victim.

The woman had called it in. She was clutching her phone in her hand as if it were a lifeline. Jo would let her. She would go at the pace the woman led. It would be the only way to get her to cooperate. Rape cases were always a delicate thing. In so many ways.

She had managed to coax the woman out of the room and to the ambulance waiting in the parking lot. She'd yet to question her, and she didn't want to even though she had to. Though she got a few basics of what occurred because she needed a starting point. Hearing the entire story would be as horrible as making the woman relive it, so she hadn't yet made the woman go word-for-word of it all. Her appearance alone was evidence that something horrible happened. Torn clothes. Bruises and scratches on her arms and face. She tried to fight back. Good for her.

"It's going to be okay," Jo reassured her as she walked her to the ambulance.

The woman had been given a blanket to cover herself. Her clothes weren't presentable, and the marks covering her body didn't need to be witnessed by everyone. It made Jo sick to her stomach. She hadn't eaten yet tonight and she doubted she would now.

"We got him. You're okay now."

The woman stopped a few feet from the ambulance. "You didn't get him."

Jo glanced at the patrol car behind the woman where the man she'd handcuffed sat in the back seat of the car.

"The man—"

The woman shook her head, swallowing hard. "It wasn't him. I don't know who he is, but he saved my life. The man..." Her bottom lip trembled. "The man stopped...there was a noise...he hit me hard in the head and got off me. Then he ran out of the room. I think the other guy chased him. I called the police as soon as the guy ran."

"They could be working together."

Tears rained down her cheeks. "It was one person who dragged me up there. Not two." Then sobs tore out of the woman and Jo let the paramedic take over. She'd try to interview the woman more after she got checked out at the hospital.

A rape kit would need to be done.

Jo made her way to the patrol car. Officer Smith stood outside near the front of it.

"Has he said anything?" Though she had read him his rights, so he didn't need to say anything. It would be in his own best interest if he didn't. But maybe one case would go super easy for her and the guy would confess everything without coaxing to do so.

Officer Smith chuckled. "One thing. To call Detective Rider."

Interesting. "And did you?"

Officer Smith winced.

Of course he did. Because why would a male officer ask her permission for anything? She was a stupid dumb blonde cop.

"I'll handle this."

The look she gave him said he was dismissed. Officer Smith wisely walked away.

Jo opened the door and got her first good look at him. She couldn't place his name, but he looked vaguely familiar.

"Oh, shit, I know you."

Obviously, he recognized her as well. But from where?

"This is a big misunderstanding. I swear I did not touch that woman. I was trying to help her."

According to the woman, he wasn't lying.

"What's your name?"

"Jason Swanson."

Jo closed the door and walked to her own vehicle where she ran his name. She still couldn't place how she knew him. Not even his name rang a bell. But he had an interesting record.

She made her way back to him, opening the door.

"You were arrested for assault and released this morning. Tell me why I should believe you did nothing to that woman."

"Okay, first off, I was defending a different woman last

night from a drunken asshole. Should I have used my fists to tell him to knock it off? I guess not. But I did nothing wrong last night. I own the construction company remodeling this building and have every right to be here. I was checking out the site when I heard a noise. I went to check it out and this guy ran out of the room. I ran after him. When I went back upstairs, I saw the woman and was about to call the police when you arrived." He jangled his wrists behind his back. "Here we are. I swear I didn't touch that woman."

His story seemed to line up with the small amount the woman had relayed.

A throat cleared behind her. She twisted to see Rider, smiling a crooked grin.

"Hey, Jo. How's it going?"

She liked Rider. He was one of the good guys at the precinct. Just like Tate. He treated her like she was normal. He'd even invited her to his wedding.

That's it!

That's where she knew this guy. He'd been the best man at Rider's wedding seven months ago.

"I've had better days."

She wasn't going to go into the shit she'd been dealing with earlier. This mayhem was adding on to a horrible day. But none of it was new in her line of work. Same shit, different day.

"Umm..." Rider glanced at his friend. "Hey, Jason. I hear you had an eventful night last night and now some more fun."

"Dude, I would not call this fun." Then Jason groaned, leaning his head on the seat in front of him.

"I don't know what happened here, Jo, but whatever it was, Jason didn't do anything."

"How do you know if you don't even know what

happened?" Just because they were good friends didn't mean a person couldn't hide a few things about themselves.

Not even family always turned out to be who someone thought they were. She'd learned what her brother had been capable of. It wasn't something she'd ever thought possible.

"I just know."

Not good enough.

"So you're aware he was arrested last night for assault?"

Rider nodded. "I am. His sister—my wife—bailed him out this morning."

"And you're trying to bail him out now? From a rape charge?"

"Woah!"

"I did not do that!"

She glanced between Rider and Jason, unbothered by their outbursts. She couldn't get riled up by things like that. Not in a male dominated world. Keeping her cool was essential to surviving.

"Look, Jo, I'm not trying to step on your toes—"

"That's exactly what you're doing. I didn't call you here. Another officer did. I didn't ask for your opinion or your help. Your friend is in trouble, and you're trying to get him out of it without the full picture."

Rider stared at his friend for a long time before bowing his head. "I apologize. You're right. May I assist you in this matter? I don't believe my friend had anything to do with it, and the faster we can clear him, the better."

Well, based on the woman's brief statement, Jo was beginning to think he didn't do anything either, but she wasn't going to let the guy off the hook that easily. She wouldn't be railroaded by a co-worker either. She appreciated that he understood that without putting up a fight.

"I take the lead on this. You can hang around in the background."

Then she shut the car door again. The man wasn't getting free until she knew for sure he had nothing to do with hurting that woman.

3

Jason slammed his apartment door harder than he intended. Now he'd get a complaint from the neighbor across the hallway—Tasha—who hated his guts. To be fair, she seemed to hate most people, so he didn't take it personally. But she loved to complain to the superintendent of the building, Harry, about the littlest infraction.

A beer sounded great right about now. But so did a shower.

The shower won.

He'd been handcuffed and stuffed into the back seat of a car twice in less than twenty-four hours. The difference between the two incidents was one time he'd been thrown in a cell afterward. This latest one he'd been shoved into an interrogation room. Both times sucked!

The hot water streamed down over him, and he could do nothing but stand there.

What the hell happened?

That's all that raced through his mind. He'd gone to work to escape and he'd fallen into another hole of despair.

Rape!

That's what he'd nearly been charged with.

He wasn't sure if Rider had pulled some strings or what, but he'd been released less than an hour ago with no charges filed. Yet. The woman detective hadn't looked happy to let him go.

Damn. He couldn't remember her name. The whole evening was a blur.

It had to be near ten o'clock and he was exhausted, yet wired with energy. Of course, his mind was racing a million miles a minute while his body shook as if he got off an exhilarating ride.

He finished showering, managing to lather himself with soap and wash his hair before exiting despite not having much energy to do so. Then he grabbed the beer calling his name.

The debate on what to eat was going full force in his brain when a knock sounded on his door. Then it opened without him answering it. Rider walked in. Thank goodness for small favors his sister didn't stroll in afterward. Damn it. He should've remembered to lock his door. That's how far gone his mind had wandered that he let something so vital to his safety slip his mind.

Rider lifted a bag. "I grabbed you a burger on the way over."

Good. Now he didn't have to make the decision on his own. He grabbed another beer, trading with Rider.

"Thanks, man."

"How you holding up?"

Jason gave a merciful laugh. "I was arrested twice today. I'm doing great." Because he'd gotten arrested at one in the morning for the bar fight. Not even a whole day had passed yet.

"It was a misunderstanding this evening. Jo was doing her job."

Jo?

No. That wasn't her name. At least, that wasn't how she'd introduced herself at Rider's wedding. What name had she given him? Damn. He wished he could remember. They didn't have a moment or anything. He recalled bumping into her, ready to get drunk so he could get his dancing feet going. He had asked her to dance. She shot him down without even an upward tilt of her lips. Then she left when work drove her away.

It was not a memorable interaction.

Neither was tonight.

"I'm sorry you had to deal with what you had to. No charges will be filed."

"Good. Because I didn't touch that woman." Jason chomped into his burger, chewing aggressively.

"She told us the same thing. She gave us a good description of the man who did. Unfortunately, your site doesn't have cameras around, so we don't have him on surveillance there. The cameras around the area picked him up, but he knew where they were located, kept his face shielded. Brazen asshole returned to the scene while all the cops were there. A sketch artist will be working with her to get a drawing of him."

Excellent. Bastards like that needed to be locked up.

Rider let him eat his burger in silence, and it didn't take long. He hadn't had much to eat all day, so he was starving. The fries disappeared just as fast. Then he chugged his beer to wash it all down. While he hadn't done much besides paperwork all day, he shouldn't have skipped every meal. He couldn't allow himself to jump into a pity party or depression like he had a year ago when he was released from the hospital.

"Junelle pissed at me?"

"For what? Being at the wrong place at the wrong time? No. She's worried about you, but she didn't want to crowd you right now."

Jason fiddled with the empty bottle. "It wasn't the wrong time. What would've happened to that woman if I hadn't gone to the site?"

"I don't want to think about it. But you're right. I'm glad you were there for her. I told Jo I'd help her with the case. Just because you're off the hook doesn't mean I'm going to stop helping. We'll get this asshole."

"I hope so. I'm installing cameras tomorrow. I should've had those already." Of course, it was an added expense to have things like that. Not that his business was hurting for money, but he had to watch what he spent and where he spent it. "Want another beer?"

Rider lifted the one he'd half-finished. "Naw, I shouldn't. Are you going to be okay? I know it was a shitty day."

"I'll be fine. Tell Junelle I'm sorry. About it all."

"She's not pissed at you." Rider slapped him on the shoulder and stood up.

That wasn't the impression Jason got this morning. But maybe the incident this evening had mellowed out her ire.

"I'll check in with you tomorrow." Then Rider left.

He grabbed another beer. To avoid a third arrest in one day, he stayed home and got drunk.

When he woke up the next morning, his head pounded like a million little elves were hammering into his skull. Another hot shower and a few pain meds later, it had lessened to about a thousand elves doing damage to his brain. He grabbed a granola bar and headed to work.

Of course, his employees had heard about what happened. How, when it had happened after work hours? He didn't know and didn't care. It was good for them to be informed of anything that happened around the area. To keep their eyes peeled for anything suspicious.

He had the security cameras installed at all entrances to the building. It would've been nice to have some inside as well, but his budget would only extend so far.

Then he jumped in with his guys and got some manual labor in. Worked his muscles and shut off his brain for a short moment in time.

By the time the day ended, he was exhausted and ready to crash. He hadn't gotten much sleep the night before. That's what happened when his life was shit and he drank too much.

The first thing he did when he got home was take another shower. Again, he let the water rain down on him for the longest time before washing himself.

He should eat, but he grabbed a beer instead. He'd downed half of it when he realized that drinking his problems away wasn't the answer. It would be the easy way to solve them. But it wasn't the smartest way.

Not wanting to waste any of the beer, he at least finished the bottle he'd grabbed before grabbing a boring water bottle.

Now what to eat?

There was a nice Mexican restaurant close to the job site. Maybe he'd grab some tacos there.

Then maybe he'd check the site to make sure all was good. He didn't want a repeat of what happened last night.

"You look exhausted. Want a mojito?" Ivy asked, lifting the current one she was drinking.

"No, thank you." All Jo wanted was a long, hot bath and to erase the day.

She'd gotten nowhere in the rape case. The woman, Rowena Anderson, while traumatized, gave a wonderful description of their suspect. A sketch artist hadn't been available today, so they didn't have a complete composite of the perp, but they would soon. It would help. The lack of cameras in the area didn't yield much results.

The woman said she met him online on a dating app. Of course, when she got her first glimpse of the guy, she realized he'd used a fake photo. One more reason why Jo didn't bother with those things. Too many creepos out there. If she couldn't find a nice guy the normal way, then she didn't want a guy in her life. She didn't need one.

They had done a rape kit and sent it to the lab. If this guy had done this before, they'd find out. Jo wasn't naive to think this had been his first time. He'd had it too planned out. This wasn't an amateur. To lure her on a date, then drag her to an empty construction site. He had to have known nobody would be there. He wouldn't have wanted to risk being caught.

Of course, they met near the construction site with the intention to eat at the Mexican restaurant nearby, but they had never made it that far. So there were no other witnesses to give a description of him.

So right now, they were in a waiting game until they had more information. Nothing new in her line of work. She had so many open cases waiting for evidence to come back or a witness to appear from somewhere it was insane.

"You look like you need one."

No, all she needed was to soak her bones.

"Rough day." Like usual.

"Tell me about it." Ivy leaned her forearms on the counter, as if eager to hear about all the horrible things Jo dealt with on a daily basis. "Come on, Jo. You internalize too much. You gotta let some of that shit out. Spill. I'll be your sounding board."

"Ivy, you don't want to hear about the rape case I have no leads on. The aggravated assault that put someone's grandpa in the ICU. Or the armed robbery of a jewelry store where a woman who was picking out her engagement ring is fighting for her life."

That was a small fraction of the cases sitting on her desk waiting to be solved.

"Why was the woman picking out the ring? Shouldn't the guy be doing that?"

That's what her roommate decided to focus on? Why was Jo even surprised?

"I don't know. They talked about getting married and then decided to go ring shopping. It was a spur of the moment thing or something. Not everyone does it the traditional way."

Why the hell did she even answer her dumb question?

She needed to be alone.

Before Ivy could ask her anything else, she left the room and went straight to the bathroom. She locked the door, not wanting to bothered by anything, and started the bath. Because Ivy didn't always understand personal space. The hot water did wonders on her body. It soaked straight to the bone, absorbing all the pain she'd dealt with that day.

Too quickly, the water grew lukewarm. Although, when she exited the bath, she realized an hour had passed. So time had gone by faster than she thought.

She locked up her service weapon, doing things backward, and then got dressed. When she reemerged in the kitchen, a mojito was sitting on the counter for her. And a plate with a sandwich.

"Drink. Eat. Relax."

Ivy could drive her up the wall. But she could also know what Jo needed even when she didn't realize she needed it.

The sandwich disappeared quickly, and the mojito as fast.

"Do you want to go out for a drink? Escape this place?"

She rarely accepted that invitation. Ivy's definition of fun and hers were so wildly different.

"I'll pass."

"Remember when I said you need to get laid? That still stands."

Jo laughed. "I remember. If it happens, it happens."

Then her mind drifted to Jason Swanson. He'd flirted with her at Rider's wedding. Had even asked her to dance. Like the nervous ninny she could be, she spouted stupid stuff and then left the party. Granted, work had needed her, but she could've ignored it. She could've participated in one dance.

Now she was glad she didn't cave in. After arresting him —well, to be fair, he didn't hurt that woman. But he had been arrested before. Three times for assault. She didn't want to date a man who had an anger problem.

Again, to be fair, he had never been found guilty for any of them. Only arrested. Innocent until proven guilty.

Ivy snapped her fingers. "Where'd you go? I lost you there for a second."

Jo blew out a breath, then let out a tiny laugh. "Okay, you want a story. Remember the cute guy I told you about from the wedding how many months ago?"

"Yeah, you flopped it like you do every single time. I swear, you're out to sabotage yourself."

That wasn't a lie. She would have to agree. She didn't consciously sabotage herself, but deep down, she knew her nerves overrode anything else.

"I arrested him yesterday for rape."

"Shut up! You dodged a bullet with that one."

Jo gritted her teeth, wincing. "He had nothing to do with it. He saved that woman from..." Hell, possible death. "He happened to be there at the right time. So now he remembers me as an awkward woman who knocked down his advances, and now a cold-hearted bitch who arrested him for a crime he didn't commit."

"Or maybe it's fate putting you in each other's paths once again."

"I love how you can go from outrage to sappy in a split second."

"It's a talent." Ivy lifted a shoulder with a cunning smirk.

"I'm hopeless. I know that. I feel like I should apologize to him. But I was doing my job." Yet, she felt bad. Maybe because he was best friends with Rider. Usually, she didn't have this deep sense of remorse for doing her job.

"Then you have nothing to apologize for. Keep doing good work. Now let's go out. I'm meeting some of my friends. You should come."

They both knew she wouldn't.

Ivy didn't push too hard and left shortly after. The apartment was too quiet. She had too much on her mind to handle the quiet.

So she changed from her PJs—a tank top and drawstring pants—to jeans and a T-shirt. She grabbed her service weapon and her badge as well. She never left her apartment without the two things, even on her off-time. She knew that was part of her problem. She didn't know how to shut off the work side of herself.

Somehow she found herself at the construction site. That case, out of all of them, was bugging her the most. Maybe because of the horror the woman went through. Maybe because she felt guilty for handcuffing the wrong man. But one more time at the scene of the crime wouldn't hurt.

Except when she tried to open the door to the building, it wouldn't budge.

Well, that was a good thing. It was secure. Jason had relayed that when he walked through the building it hadn't been locked. That he hadn't thought much about it. She wondered if he'd spoken to his employees to be more vigilant about security.

She made her way back to her car and saw a light on in the mobile office. Now was her chance to apologize. Because who else would be here this late? It had to be him.

Nerves riddled her body as she walked toward the small structure. They didn't hit her when she worked. Dealing with victims, witnesses, or even suspects came easy to her. It's when anything turned personal that her anxiety burst free. Her mind didn't know how to operate when it wasn't in work-mode. What did that say about her?

She knocked and waited for him to holler she could enter. Instead, he opened the door.

"Detective...how can I help you?"

Her lips tried to form a smile, but she knew it came out lopsided. More like a frown mixed with unease. "I didn't realize you would be here."

His brows puckered inward. "Again, my company is renovating this building. I have every right to be here."

"Yes, of course." She was already mucking this up. "Did

you know cows have best friends? They get stressed when separated."

Oh my gosh.

She did *not* just spout that nonsense. But by the surprise filtering in his expression, she said that out loud. She'd read a fascinating article about it the other day. And of course, her nerves were strung tight because she needed to do one thing and she didn't know how to do it.

"I apologize."

The confusion intensified on his face.

"I made an error yesterday, and I apologize."

His entire body relaxed. It was as if she could see the tension drain from his body. "Don't apologize. You didn't do anything wrong. How is...that woman doing?"

"Not great."

"Right. I don't know why I asked." He cleared his throat, then stepped back. "Do you want to come inside? There is a slight chill in the air."

There was. She had accomplished what she meant to do, so there was no need to further the conversation. Yet, she found herself stepping inside.

He took a seat behind a desk, and she took the one on the other side.

She glanced around the room. Awkwardness was filling the space, and she didn't know how to clear it.

She pointed at a mark on the wall. "You can take a hairdryer to that. Looks like crayon. It'll come off easily. It heats the wax and then you use hot, soapy water to get it off."

His brows reached up this time instead of down.

Yes, she was embarrassing herself with this man. Nothing new there. Same thing, different guy.

4

WELL, this was different.

He stared at the woman's vacant gaze, his hands still wrapped around her neck.

She was dead and he felt...different. More elated. More excited. Having the same woman twice before killing her was euphoric. Why had he never done this before?

Well, because he'd never been interrupted in the act. He had no choice but to run. Letting her go, the risk of her giving his description had been unavoidable. Now the police knew what he looked like. He had no doubt about that. She'd been a fighter. She had resisted him every step of the way. So he knew she would have told them what he looked like.

It sort of added to the arousing element. The risk of capture. He didn't think he'd like that kind of feeling, but it didn't bother him as much as he thought it would.

Plus, he hadn't given her a whole lot of time to tell her story. A full day of freedom, just to rip it all away.

She'd been so surprised when she stepped out of her bathroom and saw him standing in the hallway. He'd even let her get out a tiny scream before he jumped on her, covering her mouth. It had been so easy to subdue her. So, so easy.

Though he hadn't planned it, she'd had nothing on but a towel. It had made it that much easier to get what he wanted. And oh, he got what he wanted.

Twice!

Yesterday and now.

To think it was possible, with that element of risk, was so exhilarating. He'd thought the hunt to find his next prey had been the peak of the thrill. But no. This was so much better.

He'd had his fill of her, then he also had to snuff out the light in her eyes.

Now he couldn't stop staring at the empty look that gazed back at him.

He'd have to do this again.

Play a little cat and mouse.

But first. Time to clean up his mess.

He used her bathroom, but made sure to wipe down any surface he touched. And of course, take the condom with him. No need to give them any help finding out who he was.

The woman hadn't gotten very far when she ran from him. Her mangled body lay in the hallway. He couldn't leave her there. This wasn't where she was supposed to die.

He had meant to take what was rightfully his at the construction site and then kill her there. Leave no witness behind. Except that's not what happened and he had to do it in her apartment.

But he didn't like that his plan had been deviated.

And he sort of liked the idea and the thrill of messing with the police.

He'd move her body back to the original spot. Make them wonder why. There was no reason why. Just because.

Because he could.

He found one of her suitcases and stuffed her inside. They made this kind of thing look much easier in the movies. Laughter filled the room. Well, duh! They didn't actually stuff a body in a suitcase. That's what special effects were for. He knew the truth. It was damn difficult.

But doable.

He strolled out of her apartment with the suitcase. No one stopped him. No one even paid him any attention.

They never did.

Because he was invisible.

HE HADN'T BEEN sure what to make of the detective at the door. For a brief moment, he thought she was back to arrest him. Hearing her apologize had been a surprise, but unnecessary. He would never fault her for doing her job. Hell, he knew how hard Rider's job was. The things he saw and dealt with every day. How could he fault any of them for doing their job?

Then he'd invited her inside and couldn't figure out why. A darted peek at her T-shirt where her nipples had pointed daggers at him had been one reason. She was cold. Get her out of the cold.

Or she was attracted to him.

Either one was an option, and he figured since she'd dismissed him at the wedding without even blinking and arrested him yesterday for a horrible crime, it wasn't horniness hitting her.

Now he couldn't figure her out at all. The random things she kept telling him.

"Thanks. I don't own a hairdryer. But I can ask my sister

for one." Not that he cared about the marks on the wall. His secretary, Susan, sometimes brought her four-year-old to work. He figured more marks would appear, and they didn't bug him.

His gaze couldn't help but go to her shirt. Still puckered.

And he needed to get his mind out of the gutter. This woman was out of his league. Beautiful. Successful. And not afraid of anything.

He couldn't help but look over his shoulder every time he left his apartment. At least, since he'd been attacked a year ago. No woman wanted to date a scaredy-cat.

"So you—"

"I wanted—"

They both stopped speaking, waiting for the other to finish their sentence. The longer they stared, the more neither could hide their smiles.

He waved a hand at her. "Please. Go first."

"So you have a sister. She's married to Rider. I do remember you from the wedding."

"Um, yes. Junelle. I also remember you from the wedding." Victoria! That's what she'd introduced herself as. Not Jo. "I believe I asked you to dance."

Her cheeks tinted a light red. The look on her was so... odd. Yet, beautiful. This strong, bold woman could get embarrassed.

"I believe I declined."

"Well," he said with a flirtatious grin, "I like to think it wasn't a rejection. You had to leave for work."

A small grin hit her lips.

"And you said your name was Victoria. Why did Rider call you Jo?"

"My name is Victoria. My last name is Johansen. Most people, especially at work, call me Jo."

Made sense. A lot of Rider's co-workers called each other by their last name. Hell, he'd called Rider by his last name all his life. And his first name was Jack. It was weird to think of him as Jack.

"I like Victoria." It was a beautiful name. "Can I call you that?"

The beautiful smile on her face inched up a notch. "You can." Then she waved her hand. "Now your turn. What were you going to say earlier?"

Oh. That. It would bring the conversation back to something not pleasant, and they were on a good path right now.

But he also didn't want to lie.

"I wanted to let you know I did install security cameras around the property. I hate that something horrific happened here."

In a flash, her gorgeous smile vanished. "That's good. A really good idea." She stood up. "I should go. I didn't mean to bother you."

He rose as well. "Not a bother. I'll walk you out. I'm done here."

She eyed him with apprehension. Were they back to disliking each other? What was with the look?

Her vehicle was parked close to his. He gave her an awkward wave. "Drive safe."

"You too." Then her lips clamped together as if she wanted to say more but was forcing herself not to.

They had a weird relationship so far. He'd been shot down once. Then the whole arresting thing. But what the hell?

"Do you want to go out sometime? Get a drink. Eat. Coffee. Whatever. Something." *Stop talking!* Then his gaze, on their own accord, darted to her chest again. Still perky.

Maybe she noticed his glance because she twisted her body to the side so he couldn't see straight on.

"Umm...I can't. I can't date someone in an active investigation."

Then she entered her vehicle and drove off, leaving him standing there rejected for a second time. He didn't doubt her reasoning, but it didn't lessen the blow that maybe she wasn't attracted to him.

But her nipples...were perky because it was cold out and she didn't have a jacket on. No other reason but that. And what an asshole to be checking her out when they were talking about sensitive things.

He drove home and, despite knowing he shouldn't, he grabbed a beer. Then another, until he fell asleep with too many gone. In the morning, he woke up with another damn excruciating headache. It was seven thirty when his phone rang. Way too early, but again, he should be at the site by eight, so not that early.

"Boss, you might want to get here right away," Terry said in lieu of a greeting.

"What happened?"

"There's a dead body here."

Shit.

What the hell?

He was there last night. He'd walked the entire place before deciding to do some paperwork. Then Victoria showed up and he left with her. They left around nine? He didn't check the exact time.

"I'm on my way."

When he got there, the place was swarming with police vehicles. He saw Rider and Victoria by the entrance to the building. Not good. Not good at all to see both of them.

"What's going on? Terry called me."

Victoria couldn't even look him in the eye. Rider had a hard time as well.

"Am I about to get arrested again for something?"

"No!" Victoria touched his arm. A jolt of electricity zapped him. She must've felt the same thing because she snatched her hand back.

Static energy?

Or intense attraction?

Did it matter?

"I do not believe you had anything to do with this. But this location seems to be a target. The woman—" She swallowed hard. "The woman who was attacked here has been found dead. Same room as the original attack."

Jason shoved his hands in his hair, closing his eyes. No. This was not happening. He saved her. He stopped the man from hurting her further.

"Jason—"

"I'll check my security cameras." His eyes popped open, cutting off Rider. Then he stalked away toward his office building.

He entered the building, not even offering Susan a small grin. And he should've. "Go home, Susan. Nothing is going to get done today. I'll call you later."

She touched his shoulder with a tired twist of her lips and left. Rider and Victoria filled the space. He booted up his computer and logged into the security system. "I did a walkthrough when I returned here around seven. Everything looked good. I didn't see anything out of the ordinary. I think we left about nine-ish." He looked at Victoria for confirmation.

She nodded.

Rider glanced between the two of them. "Why were you here, Jo?"

"Following up on a few things. Don't you revisit crime scenes?"

"Of course." Then Rider produced a shit-eating grin.

What was with the grin on his best friend's face? Ugh. He didn't have time to interpret it. There was no way in hell he'd admit he'd asked her out and got shot down. Ignoring the tension in the room, he started looking at the video around nine. He finally got a hit around eleven.

"Holy shit! Come look."

They crowded around his computer. Rider on his left with Victoria on his right. Another tiny charge hit his body when her boob brushed his shoulder as she leaned closer. And damn! She smelled good. A lavender aroma filled his senses. What was it from? He wanted to know, but not enough to ask. Right now wouldn't be the best time to ask such a question either.

They watched as a man with a hat covering his features well picked the lock on the door and then pulled something out of his trunk. A suitcase. Odd. He then disappeared inside the building for about twenty minutes before reappearing with the suitcase and driving off. The plates weren't visible, and the cameras never got a clear picture of his face. But it looked like the same build as the guy he'd chased.

"He's smart. It's as if he knew the cameras had been installed." Rider swore under his breath. "He must've killed her somewhere else and dumped her here. But why?"

"Play it again please."

She was still leaning into him. Her request felt like it had been whispered into his ear. Her mouth so close to his neck.

He needed to get his mind out of the gutter and focus on the task at hand. The video replayed and he saw nothing new that would help them.

Victoria backed away. "Can I have a copy of that?"

"Of course." He wasn't sure how to do that, but he'd figure it out. Then he twisted around. "You got a sketch of him from her. You can use that to find him, right?"

"The sketch artist hadn't met with her yet. We don't have a full picture of him. Only his description."

"Which was why he went back and killed her." Here Jason thought he'd saved this woman's life.

She touched his shoulder. "Thank you for installing the cameras. I will find something on this video that will help us find him."

Jason knew he should focus on anything but her soft touch. But he couldn't. The longer her hand stayed there, the more he wished she hadn't turned him down last night.

"Are you sure you didn't get a better look at him?"

God, he wished he had.

"I only saw the back of him. Maybe a sideview when he darted out of the room, but it was so quick, there's no way I can give you an accurate description. I'm sorry."

"Not your fault." Then her hand fell away.

He missed her touch.

"Unfortunately, this area is a crime scene. You won't be able to resume operations right now."

Yeah, he figured.

"Find this asshole. That's all I care about."

WHAT WAS SHE DOING? Touching Jason. Leaning into him. She'd told him they needed to keep things professional between them, and she meant it. Yet, she found herself needing to touch him. To be near.

Maybe because she had wanted to say yes to him last

night. She had wanted to see where the mutual attraction between them could go.

Ivy wasn't wrong when she said she needed to get laid. It had been a while. Too long. Her last boyfriend had been a dud. If one could call a three-month relationship that consisted of a total of five dates, a boyfriend. Work had impeded so many things between them that they rarely saw each other. When they did, she didn't feel a whole lot of chemistry. She'd slept with him on the last date, hoping the chemistry would burst free, except nothing but disappointment hit her. She assumed he felt it too because he never called again, and she didn't feel bothered by it. That was over eight months ago. He should've been her date at the wedding. Instead, she went solo and left early.

None of this mattered. Work came first. Always.

She and Rider had already examined the body. Rowena had been raped again. Then the man had strangled her with his bare hands, if the marks on her neck were any indication. No doubt, he'd done it right after he violated her.

But why bring her back here? It made no sense.

The room looked exactly the way it was when she had first been attacked. No one had been in there to resume any work. Maybe because it had been tainted with violence, no one wanted to enter it right away. Still. Forensics were combing the area once again for evidence.

She and Rider decided to check her apartment. It had been easy enough to get someone to open her door. Nothing looked disturbed. Except she found a broken nail in the hallway. A press-on.

She crouched, staring at it. "Is she missing a nail? Could he have attacked her here?"

"Let me make a call."

She didn't move as Rider talked on the phone. This poor

woman. Dealing with the aftermath of a violating attack, only to be attacked again and then murdered. Jo should've done more. She should've figured out the man who attacked her would come back to silence her. She'd seen his face. Of course she'd be in danger.

Yet, so many women were hurt in the same manner and not all perpetrators came back to kill them. How could she have known this would happen?

"She is missing a nail."

Jo stood up, acknowledging she heard him with a quick bob of her head. She didn't have to tell Rider to send forensics here when they were done at the other location. He would have told them that.

They found a black suitcase, like the one in the video, in the woman's closet.

"Did he return the suitcase? Or did he bring his own?"

Rider stood next to her as they stared intently at the black device. "That's a great question. Forensics will let us know. I don't get why he moved her body to begin with."

"Well, when we find him, we'll ask." Because she would get this guy. He wouldn't hurt anyone else. She couldn't allow it.

They found the super again, this time requesting access to the cameras in the lobby. No other security system was in place in the building. They took copies of the video where the man was seen leaving the building with a suitcase and returning with it. They even found when he first arrived, before he killed her. Every time he shielded his face with the ball cap. He was smart enough to know where the cameras were located.

How?

Had he cased the place before? Did he know where

cameras were usually installed? Not every building was the same.

Overall, it told Jo this man had been at this game for a long time. He wasn't a new offender.

She and Rider spent the day interviewing Rowena's friends and family. Trying to piece together more of her movements. None of it helped them get closer to a suspect.

Even the dating app angle was useless. His name and all the information on his profile were fake, even the picture. Because the photo online didn't match the description the woman had given them. The victim had even mentioned how the moment she realized they didn't match, she tried to walk away. That's when he'd turned violent. Grabbed her and dragged her to the construction site. The profile had been nothing but a lure so he could hurt her. They requested a warrant from the company for his legal information, but Jo had her doubts on that as well. Hopefully, it would at least yield his IP address and they could trace his location based off his profile. No doubt, nothing useful would come back because this guy seemed so smart. She wouldn't hold her breath for anything.

Of course, forensics did their job collecting evidence. But it would be a while before they heard anything back. The lab was so behind. Her case wasn't any more important than any other cases. At least, not to the lab. To her, it was.

"Go home, Jo. Get some rest."

She looked up from her desk at Rider. "In a little bit. Thanks for your help today."

"I'm sorry we didn't uncover more. It's not your fault what happened. That he returned to hurt her."

She hadn't voiced she thought it was her fault, but obviously it had been written on her face. Either that or he figured she did because he would think it was his fault too if he'd been in her shoes. She was the lead detective on it. She should've seen this coming.

"Do you want to come over for supper?"

"I'll be fine, Rider. Thank you for the concern. Have a good night, and tell Junelle I said hello."

Rider smiled and turned to walk away.

"Oh, and tell her I'm sorry I arrested her brother." She didn't know why she even added that, but she still felt bad about it. Jason had been nothing but helpful since this all started.

Rider twisted back her way. "You were doing your job. No one faults you for that either. Jason's a good guy."

"I believe that."

The weird grin on Rider's face sent a shot of nerves to her gut. "Well, have a good night, *Jo*."

She stared at his back, wondering why he emphasized her name.

Whatever. She didn't want to think about Jason or anything but how she could find a suspect in this murder.

She went over the videos from Rowena's apartment and the construction site until her eyes started blurring.

That was her cue it was time to go home.

Ivy wasn't around when she got there, and as horrible as the thought rolled through her mind, she was glad. Dealing with Ivy could be a trial at times. Her mind and body were exhausted from the day.

She took a bath, letting the hot water soak into her bones until the water grew lukewarm. As usual. Though when she got out, she didn't feel any better than when she'd gotten in. She put on a tank top and draw string pants when a knock sounded on her door.

Odd.

So someone got into the building without buzzing her apartment first.

A quick peek through the peephole had her backing up a step.

Jason stood on the other side. How did he know where she lived? And why was he here?

One way to find out.

She opened the door.

His intense stare had her insides melting with desire. She could feel her nipples perking to attention. Like last night. His gaze trailed there for a split second, then back to her face. Her cheeks tinted red.

Then she snapped out of her dazed pleasure. What was he doing here?

"Are you stalking me?"

5

Gosh, that sounded harsh. She hadn't meant to sound that way. By the way he flinched, she'd put a wide divider between them again.

"Umm, no. I'm sorry to show up like this. Rider gave me your address."

Did he now?

Why would he do that?

She needed to calm herself down. She knew Jason wasn't a bad guy, like Rider had said. But he made her very nervous. She hadn't felt this kind of attraction to a man in a long time. Flirting and dating and putting herself out there always made her awkward.

"I'll go."

Jason was halfway down the hallway when she stuck her head out. "Stop. You came for a reason. Come on in."

She was a detective first and foremost. She would keep this strictly professional. Jason didn't strike her as the kind of guy who couldn't take no for an answer. Which meant he was here for a different reason.

"I can come by the precinct tomorrow. It's fine."

See. She knew it. He hadn't come to ask her out again. It was related to the case. Why did the thought disappoint her?

"No. It was important enough to come tonight, so tell me now."

Though, he had to have called Rider to get her address. Why didn't he tell Rider?

Jason moved toward her door, stepping inside with apprehension. He even jumped when she closed the door, and she hadn't slammed it or anything. Very odd. Maybe he was nervous as well. But why? It was work-related.

"Have a seat." She waved a hand at a stool at the island counter. "I haven't eaten yet. Do you want something to eat?"

Now why did she offer that? She should find out what he wanted and get him the hell out of her place.

"Yeah, sure." Jason took a seat, avoiding eye contact.

Definitely nervous.

"So tell me why you're here," she said as she prepared two sandwiches. Something quick and easy.

"I was thinking about that guy...trying to remember as much as I could about him. I want to help catch him. I didn't get a full view of his face, but I did see his side profile. Kind of. I thought maybe I could work with the sketch artist. With what the woman told you and with the little I can give, maybe we can get a good sketch of this guy."

It wasn't a bad idea. It might not yield the best results, but it was better than nothing.

"Okay. It can't hurt." It did not require a visit to her apartment though. "Was that all?"

He shrugged. "Yeah. It kind of was. I..." He looked away toward the door as if he were thinking about fleeing. Then his dark-blue eyes met hers again. She'd never noticed the color of his eyes before. They were darker than she'd ever seen blue eyes be. Maybe because they were full of despair. She knew that feeling well.

"I'm sorry about what happened to her. I feel...I don't know. I can't believe she's gone."

She pushed his plate near him. "I understand everything you're feeling. It's normal, Jason. I feel guilty about it as well. That I should've done more to help her. This world is a very vicious place. I've seen so much horrible things that it doesn't surprise me anymore."

Silence filled the room.

Maybe because there wasn't anything else to say. They both understood where the other was coming from. She didn't question him coming over anymore. He wasn't used to this kind of violence in his life, and she recognized the need for him to understand it more.

Though, he wasn't completely innocent of violence. He had been stabbed and nearly died. She'd heard all about it at the precinct. Even offered words of encouragement to Rider, though he'd been in a bad place at the time, getting hurt himself not too long before that.

So much violence.

So much pain.

When would it all stop?

Jason rubbed his hands together, removing the crumbs. "That was delicious. I skipped lunch, so that hit the spot. Thank you."

"You're welcome." The moment went from professional to personal in an instant, which of course, made her nerves spring free. She had no idea what to say. Where to go from here.

"Did you know that a hummingbird weighs less than a penny? The bee hummingbird weighs less than two grams and a penny weighs about two point five grams."

A crooked grin touched his lips. "I did not know that. It's kind of crazy to think about and picture. A hummingbird is still larger than a penny, so that's kind of cool to think it weighs less."

A smile burst free on her as her stomach twirled in somersaults. Instead of looking at her funny or dismissing her, he engaged with her ridiculous topic. Not many people humored her in moments like this.

More silence coated the air, but unlike last time, they stared at each other with goofy grins.

"I like to watch documentaries and stuff. There's so many interesting things you can learn." She avoided his gaze as she reached for his plate and then stacked it on top of hers. They hit the sink with a quiet clink. "After a long, crappy day, I like to absorb the opposite of what I deal with every day. It doesn't always help remove the nasty things I see, but, well, I learn a lot of new stuff."

She never told people this. Ivy loved to roll her eyes and laugh at her when she saw the things she liked to watch. Of course, Ivy was the complete opposite of her. She'd never be caught dead watching a documentary on whales or dolphins or the life of an insect.

"I wouldn't mind watching something like that."

She swiveled around from the sink, his midnight-blue eyes staring at her so intently, it's as if she was looking at herself in the mirror. His eyes reflected everything she felt the past few days. Heartache. Despair. Sorrow. Deep, deep pain that couldn't be described.

"I think it's an episode on bugs tonight. The walking stick bug to be exact."

Jason flickered a glance at her couch. "Can I join you?"

Things were supposed to be professional between them. Nothing more.

Yet, the eagerness in his eyes, the fact he kept turning out to be something she didn't expect, had her nodding.

"Do you want a drink?"

He stood. "Not really." Then his brows drew inward. "I hate to admit that I've turned to the bottle a little too much. I don't want to form a bad habit."

Talk about being real and raw with her. He didn't have to admit that. She would've never been the wiser.

They ventured to her living room and took a seat on the couch. A bit of distance between them, but not too much where, if she put her arm out to the side, she'd be able to touch him.

She found the channel she wanted, then the narrator droned on about a bug that fascinated her. Because it was something other than violence and death.

As the night wore on, the distance between them closed inch by inch, so by the time the episode finished, his thigh was touching hers.

THE DOOR SHUT WITH A THUD. Not quite a slam, but not gentle either. His mistake. But his nerves were on edge.

He walked into the kitchen, smiling at his sister who was rolling out dough.

"What are you making?"

Her brow cocked as she stopped her movements. "What's wrong?"

A very loaded question. One he would never answer. His sister, May, wouldn't understand the torment inside him. Nobody could.

"Bad day at work. You know how it is." He leaned on the counter, staring at the dough. "What are you making?"

She pinned a hard stare at him, then resumed her activity. "Bunny sugar cookies. It's almost Easter and the kids love when I bring in treats."

His sister was a kindergarten teacher, and he had no idea how she had the patience to deal with kids that age. He'd go insane.

"Do I get to taste test them?" He made sure to offer the sweetest smile in his arsenal. The ones his sister could never say no to.

Or any woman, for that matter. He just had that kind of charm.

"Only one." She wagged her finger at him, laughing, knowing quite well he'd have at least two or three. He knew she'd make enough for him to steal even a few more than that.

"How did your date go the other night?"

Horrible. Not at all how he had planned it, but he'd solved that little dilemma.

"It didn't work out."

May stopped the rolling pin again. "Well, tell me about it? What went wrong?"

Where did he start? Some asshole interrupted him in the throes of his passion, making him flee the scene. Then the woman had a chance to give a description to the police. Of course, he fixed his mistake by taking care of her. What an eye-opener that was, realizing how exhilarating it could be taking the same woman twice. The fear. The horror in her eyes. The risk involved. Then finding the sketch of him hanging up in the precinct.

When he'd seen the flyer hanging on the wall, he nearly turned around and fled. But that would've raised red flags. That would've been careless. So he continued on his way, completed his job, and left as if he had no worries in the world.

Except he did.

The woman had given a decent description. The artist who captured his likeness had talent. He could only hope no one put two and two together.

"She wasn't the one. Okay, sis. We didn't have much chemistry. What can I say? The spark wasn't there."

May had moved on to the bunny cookie cutter, pressing it into the dough over and over. "I know someone you would have a spark with."

"Nope." He shook his head, laughing. "You're not setting me up."

Because she'd done that before and it never worked out. Why would it? He had expectations when it came to women, and each and every one of them always fell short. He doubted he'd ever find his true soulmate out there.

Not that he believed in soulmates.

Women were good for one thing—to pleasure him.

Of course, he'd never tell his sister something grotesque like that. She'd be appalled, and the last thing he wanted was to hurt his sister. She was the one woman in the world he loved. No doubt, would ever love.

"She's sweet. Really beautiful. I know you two would hit it off." May rolled her eyes. "You're never going to find a decent woman on those stupid dating apps."

To be fair, he wasn't looking for a decent woman on the apps. Just his next prey.

"One date. We can make it a double date." She jumped up and down, clapping her hands, then left them clasped together in the gesture of a prayer.

That was the thing about his sister.

He could never tell her no.

Or disappoint her in any way.

"Okay, fine. One date. And I prefer it not be a double date. I never like the guys you hook up with."

And he'd never confess some of the things he'd done to a few of her past boyfriends. He knew they'd never tell her either. Hell, some of them were six feet under. Kind of hard talk when they were dead.

She mock pouted. "Hey, this new guy Jerry is pretty great. I think you'll like him." She transferred the bunnies to a cookie pan. "And he's a cop. Can't get much safer than that. Because I know how much you worry about me."

Well, shit.

"Twist my arm." He chuckled. "Okay, let's do a double date."

He wasn't about to leave his sister alone with a cop.

Maybe he could extract some information from him.

How much did the police know? They had a decent sketch of him, but the bigger question was, did they have more evidence?

6

Jason walked through the precinct, smiling and waving at people. He knew most of them, but only through Rider, so it wasn't as if he knew them very well. Some he liked, and some he wished he'd never met.

The one coming his way, he'd take a bullet for. Though he hoped that never happened. Getting injured and stuck in the hospital for as long as he had never needed to happen again.

"Hey, man," Rider said, clapping him on the back. "What are you doing here?"

He wasn't sure how to answer that.

The episode on the walking bug had been far more entertaining than he thought it'd be, especially since he didn't watch documentaries and such. But what had been even more mind boggling had been how comfortable he felt sitting next to a woman and simply sharing the space with her. Words weren't spoken and it hadn't mattered. The tension had disappeared. His worries, for a brief moment in time, had vanished. For once, he'd relaxed and enjoyed the moment.

That had been three days ago.

In that timeframe, he'd spoken to a sketch artist and given his—rather lame—description of the suspect.

His construction site was still off-limits, and understandably so. Though, pretty soon he would need to start back up production.

That was a good reason to be here.

But he was here for a completely different reason, even though he knew he'd never voice it out loud.

Victoria.

He missed her. He missed the sense of contentment he'd felt three nights ago. He wanted it back. But of course he couldn't find the nerve to knock on her apartment door again. She hadn't been by to see him either.

"I'm checking in on the investigation. I mean, I know how these things work. It takes time, but..." He shrugged. What else could he say? He had no good reason to be here.

"Jo's at her desk." Rider tossed his head in the direction he could find her. "I have to run though. I'm working on something else. Dinner later this week?"

"Yeah, sure, man."

Then Rider was walking away and he had no choice but to move forward. Especially if he didn't want to look odd standing in the middle of the hallway.

He smiled and waved again to a few more people he knew. Stromberg and Tate were hunched together at their desks, so they didn't see him, but he'd stop by before he left. Out of all of Rider's co-workers, he knew those two the best. Good guys. Ones he'd want in his corner for anything.

His heart rate sped up as he approached Victoria's desk. She looked up from her paperwork before he had a chance to speak. But he threw out a warm grin.

"Jason," she cleared her throat. "Hello. Hi. How are you?"

"Fine. And you?"

Awkward.

Where was the ease they conversed with a few nights ago? The comfort? The feeling they'd known each other forever?

"Yes. Good. Fine. Yes." She cleared her throat again. "Did you know that cats can't move their jaw sideways? Like we can. Which is amazing. They can only move it up and down."

A random fact.

He could work with a random fact.

"And their nose prints are unique. No cat has the same kind of nose print. It's like fingerprints with us."

The most gorgeous smile lit up her face. "Did you watch that episode last night?"

Guilty as charged.

Because he missed her, and like the coward he was, he couldn't find the nerve to go to her place again. While he had her phone number, because he'd weaseled it out of Rider, he'd felt odd calling her out of the blue.

Hell, he'd asked her out twice, and been rejected twice. He didn't think she'd want him to text her out of nowhere.

"Yeah, some of it." He'd never admit he watched the entire episode.

The smile on her face brightened even more. Then she gestured at a chair. "Please, have a seat."

So far, so good.

"I wanted—"

"Did you—"

They both laughed. They had a funny habit of interrupting each other.

"You go first." She gestured again, pointing at him, then relaxed in her chair.

"Umm...okay. I wanted to know how the...case is progressing."

Lies.

He cared, of course. It would be pretty shitty of him if he didn't, but that hadn't been the real reason he showed up. He'd found the courage to see her again, and the case was his excuse for doing so.

"It's not progressing much. We're still waiting on forensics for a few things." The happiness she displayed earlier dimmed to nothing. "I don't have high hopes much will come back in our favor. This guy, I believe, is a pro. He knows what he's doing." She reached out like she was going to touch his hand, but stopped herself at the last second. "I appreciate you working with the sketch artist. We have his face hanging up everywhere, so maybe that'll pan out. It was a huge help."

"Great. I'm glad. If I can help in any other way, just ask."

"Of course." Her hand slithered back toward her side of the desk. "You should be cleared to resume operations by the end of the week. I think forensics is finished. Let me confirm first. I'm sorry things have taken so long. I will get back to you soon about all of it."

A woman was dead. He wasn't too concerned about the job.

"It's fine. I understand."

"Good. Great."

This time he gestured toward her. "And what were you going to say?"

"Oh." She giggled, swiping a hand across her forehead and behind her ear as if pulling imaginary hair out of the way. Her beautiful blonde locks were pulled back in a tight ponytail. Not a strand was out of place.

Three nights ago was the first time he'd seen it down. It

had been wet too, as if she'd just gotten out of the shower. Of course, it didn't matter how she wore her hair, she was beautiful. Every interaction with her made her that much more gorgeous in his eyes.

"Did you eat lunch yet?" Her throat cleared again. "Because I was on my way out soon. If you wanted to join me."

His silent prayers he said at night before he went to bed were being answered.

"I could eat. Yeah. I'd love to eat. With you."

"Great. Good."

She stood up and he followed suit.

If their conversation continued with such awkwardness, it was going to be a very long lunch. And it didn't bother him one bit. Because at least they were nervous together.

Wow. This man.

She'd never had anyone, not even a friend, who enjoyed the same kind of shows she did. And a guy? None of them ever indulged her in her interests. So for Jason to watch the same episode last night, without her even knowing, it hit her square in the chest. In a place she'd never been hit before.

Why had he watched it? It couldn't be something he normally did. It didn't seem his style.

It didn't matter.

What counted was the fact he did and shared his own fact instead of laughing at hers.

They walked out of the precinct in silence. The awkwardness that had appeared in the beginning remained, though she tried to ignore it.

There was a diner not too far away, so she headed in that

direction. Jason followed without asking where they were going.

She liked that about him. That he didn't feel the need to take over the situation and make the decisions. He was leaving it all up to her.

Maybe that's why she asked if he wanted to grab lunch. She'd been afraid he wouldn't try asking her out again. Not when she'd declined the last time by giving him a pretty good reason why they shouldn't go out.

That reason remained.

Dating someone involved in one of her cases was never good. And borderline unethical. Of course, he wasn't a victim. He wasn't a suspect. At most, he was a witness. The rate the case was going, she wasn't going to get the perp. Another victim with no closure. It happened. It was a part of life. The very unfortunate part.

Was she supposed to keep Jason out of her life forever, if that were the case?

Did that seem fair to her? To him?

She didn't have a clear answer to that, and maybe she should've given it more time.

But she didn't.

The question popped out, and here they were. Walking side by side to their first...date?

No. Simply lunch.

Because if one wanted to count their interactions as a date, three nights ago would count as the first one. Unofficially, anyway.

But she wasn't counting, so therefore, this was having lunch with a friend. A new friend. A friend she was attracted to and wondered on more than one occasion what it would be like to kiss him.

But a friend, nonetheless.

Silence remained the entire way. Which was fine. She didn't always need noise or meaningless words to fill the space. It also gave her the opportunity to notice the way he walked. Rigid in every single way. His entire body was coiled tight with tension. She didn't think it had to do with her, especially when she saw him glance from side to side, and even at times behind him. As if needing to be prepared for someone to attack.

Every time they came to a corner, not that there were many, he slowed down, as if anticipating something would jump out at them. He took his time approaching it, glancing quickly to his right and left, then continued on at a normal pace.

She said nothing about the behavior. Because she understood it. It wasn't the first time she'd seen a victim of an attack react in such ways. And that's what Jason was—a victim. Brutally attacked with a knife on the open street. It had come out of nowhere. Even for a strong man like him, it could shake a person to the core. Who was she to question his behavior or his actions.

The last thing she knew he would want was for her to feel sorry for him. She dismissed the notion and pretended like she wasn't seeing a thing.

Jason held open the door for her and even pulled out her chair before sitting down himself. Such a gentlemen. Not all men did that for her when she went out. Perhaps that's why she didn't continue dating them, among other reasons.

The waitress took their drink order, left menus on the table, and walked away.

"How late did you stay up?" She glanced at him, then at the menu, wondering why, after such a long silence between them, she started with that. "I mean, did you stay up to watch the episode on otters?"

"I would like to say yes. Technically, I did." A sheepish grin touched his lips. "I might've fallen asleep halfway through the cat episode. I woke up two hours later. Turned the TV off and dragged myself to bed. So if the TV on counts as watching it, yes, I did."

She laughed. "I'm going with that doesn't count. You have to be watching it."

"Fair enough. Does it air again soon? I'll watch it then."

She bit her bottom lip, turning her gaze away from his penetrating stare, back to her menu.

What was she doing?

Either going all in here, or walking away after this impromptu lunch.

"That's the nice thing about streaming services and such these days. You can watch anything you want over and over again. The episode is available whenever you want to watch it."

Her gaze darted back up to him. That same deep, longing stare held her captive. Maybe it was how he looked at her. Or maybe it was the same longing she felt in the pit of her stomach. The words popped out without thinking.

"I wouldn't mind watching it again. If you want company, that is."

His entire face lit up with pleasure. It made that funny, exhilarating feeling in her stomach soar to an even crazier frenzy.

"I'd love company. I can't wait to learn more about otters."

They were adorable creatures.

But so was the man sitting across from her.

A man that continued to surprise her with every interaction.

The waitress returned, taking their orders. She had barely glanced at her menu, and when she did, her eyes didn't retain anything she read. She went based off memory, getting one of the usual things she ordered when she ate at the diner. Turkey club sandwich with a bag of plain potato chips on the side instead of fries.

From there, the conversation turned smoother, less awkwardness on both sides. Her nerves dissipated with rapid ease. Jason made it easy to forget why she should be worried about anything.

Right as their food arrived, her phone went off.

"Sorry. Excuse me for a moment." Life as a detective didn't give her the luxury of ignoring phone calls. This one was no different.

After speaking to the person on the other end, her stomach reactivated its activity, doing somersaults and wringing her emotions dry.

"I'm so sorry, Jason. I have to go. I'll have to take my food to go. Of course you can stay here and eat. Or take yours to go too. But I—"

Jason reached out, placing his hand over hers. The gentle smile he wore eased some of the discomfort filling her up. "It's okay. You're on the clock. Work calls. I get it. Maybe we can try again tonight with supper. And eat together."

She would love that.

And she wished her job meant she clocked in and out on regular times, but her phone went off at all hours of the day. Even in the middle of the night. When it went off, she responded. There was no 'on-the-clock' for her. Unless one considered twenty-four-seven on-the-clock.

"I would like that. I'll call you later."

"That works."

She asked for a to-go box, not surprised when Jason also requested one. He paid the bill, though she had offered to pay for it. She had been the one to suggest they eat.

He walked outside with her and even joined her on the small trek back to the precinct. Of course he did, especially if he drove there. He needed his vehicle. Unless he took public transportation of some kind. But doubtful. She'd seen his truck. Why would he take the subway or something when he had his own vehicle?

And she was getting sidetracked because they were about to part ways and she didn't know what to say. Or what he might do.

It wasn't a date. At least, she had classified it as not a date. So therefore, he couldn't kiss her.

Yet, she wanted one.

But outside the precinct wasn't a great idea either.

She'd been waging an intense war in her mind, she didn't realize Jason didn't follow her up the stairs to the door. Of course, why would he? His business was completed. Hers wasn't.

"Until tonight, Victoria." He offered a short wave, a tender upward twist of his lips, and then headed back the way they'd come from.

Interesting.

He didn't need to walk all the way back, but he had. For her.

This man.

She could fall way too fast for him if she wasn't careful.

7

JASON SCRUBBED hard on the counter, to the point his fingers ached. Then he flinched when a knock sounded on his door.

He opened it up to his sister.

"Can I come in?" she asked with a chuckle when he stood there and stared at her.

"Uh, yeah."

Then he retreated back to the kitchen to finish what he'd been doing. Cleaning his apartment from top to bottom. Every speck of dusk. Every cobweb. Every little dirty mark he saw, he wiped it away.

"What's going on?" Junelle frowned as his agitated movements on the counter were a dead giveaway.

He cleaned like a maniac when he was stressed.

"I can't get this salsa stain out of the counter. It's bugging me."

Junelle leaned closer, laughing. "I don't see anything. I think you got it."

When he took another look, he had to admit she was right.

"So what's up, sis?"

Because he had too much to do right now. She better make it quick.

"I can't visit my favorite brother?"

That garnered a chuckle out of him. "I'm your only brother."

"I haven't heard from you in a week. I wanted to check on you. Rider said you're fine, but...we always talk, and it's odd we haven't in the past week."

He had no good excuse for that.

In the past three months, when a woman was murdered at one of his sites, his life had changed. Drastically.

Thank goodness he could say it changed for the better.

He wasn't looking over his shoulder as much. He couldn't even say when that had stopped, but he didn't feel the need to be vigilant as much as before. The pain in his side didn't flair up like it used to. Maybe because he'd taken to working out more religiously than before. He'd toned down his drinking—by a lot.

And he'd started dating the most wonderful woman he'd ever met.

Victoria.

While it hadn't been puppies and roses the whole time, he enjoyed the time he spent with her.

She worked. A lot. There were times they set a date and she had to leave in the middle of it. He didn't let it bother him because he understood the kind of job she had. He'd seen Rider do the same thing on numerous occasions.

So when they were together and it wasn't interrupted, he enjoyed every single moment of it. Tonight, he had planned a romantic dinner. Something to show her how much he cared about her. That he enjoyed their time together.

And maybe, just maybe, they might take their relationship to another level. To the bedroom. If he was lucky.

If it didn't happen, he wouldn't fret about it. Because he liked Victoria too much to ruin the good thing they had going. He was attracted to her, but he also enjoyed her company. She was easy to talk to, and he felt like she understood him more than most people did. Sometimes, even his sister.

"Jason?" She snapped her fingers in front of his face when he didn't respond. "Are you okay?"

"I'm fine." Other than the fact he was hoping to sleep with his girlfriend for the first time tonight.

Well, he assumed Victoria was his girlfriend. They hadn't talked about exclusivity or anything, but they were together so often, what else could he call her? Of course they were dating.

Unless she only thought of him as a friend. A good friend she saw all the time. Kissed on occasion.

No. They were dating.

So yeah, she was his girlfriend. End of story.

"It's not like you to not keep in contact with me."

He grinned, shaking his head. "Junelle, I had a busy week at work and that's it. I'm sorry I didn't reach out."

She looked at his counter. "And busy cleaning like a freak. What's got you in a mood?"

Why hide it from her? Maybe she'd have some good insight.

"Victoria's coming over tonight and I want it to be perfect."

"How are things going with you and her?" A crafty smirk lit up her face. "I'm so happy to see you dating a normal human for once."

Yeah, he wouldn't disagree he'd dated a few doozies.

Ones he should've passed on from the moment of hello. But sometimes you had to dig through the pile to find a gem.

"Good. Really good. I mean, her work can get crazy, but I get it. I enjoy spending time with her. I wanted to treat her to a nice dinner tonight and get her to relax. She's been working on a few tough cases lately."

All the time was more like it. Crime never stopped, and he swore Victoria always got the worst of the worst. Not that she talked about her cases with him. He sensed it.

He knew it weighed on her that she hadn't found the culprit who'd raped and murdered that woman. It weighed on him too. To think he'd been so close to saving her for it all to be ripped away in the end.

"That's sweet of you. I'm sure she'll appreciate it. I get it. Rider's job takes a lot out of him. They need moments like this. I'm sure whatever you do will be perfect." Junelle reached out, covering his hand. "You don't need to stress yourself out like this. You've been seeing her for three months. She doesn't need you to be anything but what you've been being. You."

Easier said than done. Junelle had no idea he was hoping to move the relationship into new territory. And talking about sex with his sister was not a topic he wanted to have.

This was the first relationship he'd ever had where he'd waited so long to have sex. He wasn't sure why. There were times he thought it could've heated up and turned super physical, but then the moment always died before they got there. While they'd kissed a few times, they were always light and carefree. Nothing that said let's dive into the bedroom for more.

He'd never understood the term blue balls until now.

"I was going to make Mom's lasagna recipe. Too messy?"

"No, it's delicious. She'll love it. She'll love anything you make because not every guy can cook. Do you want my help with anything?"

No. He wanted to do this all on his own.

"As much as I appreciate it, I want to do this myself."

She squeezed his hand. "Okay. I'll check in with you tomorrow to see how it all went. Good luck." Junelle headed for the front door. "Oh, and I want to meet Victoria. I know she was at our wedding, but I don't remember everyone. So I'd love to have both of you over sometime."

"Yeah, okay."

One thing at a time.

First sex. Then meet the family.

Junelle left and Jason went right back to cleaning like a demon had possessed him. After that, he started cooking and setting the table. Candles to set the mood. Light, sappy music in the background. He showered and dressed up more than he normally did. Slacks with a light-blue sweater. If the candles and music didn't give her a clue he was trying to woo her, his clothes would. He never dressed up to this extent. He was more of a jeans and T-shirt kind of guy.

Twenty more minutes and she'd arrive.

He rubbed his hands on his pants, trying to dispel the sweat accumulating. Junelle was right. He had to be himself. He was putting too much stock in this evening. If they didn't venture to his room, no big deal. It wouldn't be the end of the world.

He liked Victoria. Way too much to push her away if she wasn't ready for sex.

"Oh, la, la," Ivy drawled as Jo walked into the kitchen. "Someone has a hot date tonight. How is Jason? That scrumptious man."

She chuckled, though didn't disagree with her assessment. He was a very scrumptious man. Sweet, attentive, and hot as sin. The fact he was single when she met him amazed her. He should've been snatched up ages ago. When they first started hanging out, she wondered when she would find out the reason he was single. That one thing that turned women away.

Yet, she never saw anything.

He opened doors for her. He listened to her, even when she spouted her crazy facts. Hell, he even watched the documentaries she loved, soaking up all the information with her instead of teasing her about it. There were times he told a random fact, and she loved that about him.

She couldn't find one thing wrong with him.

They'd grown very close in the last three months.

But not as close as she had hoped.

They still hadn't had sex. She wasn't sure if that was because of something she was doing wrong or he wasn't attracted to her. Or maybe he didn't want to get trapped with a woman who constantly left his side. Her job had torn her away from him one too many times. She was embarrassed thinking about it. So she didn't blame him if he didn't want to take it to the next level.

Since she didn't want to ruin the good thing they had going, she never brought it up. With her luck, he'd tell her this wasn't working for him and they shouldn't see each other anymore.

"He's making me supper tonight. I don't usually dress up. Is it too much? We're always casual with each other." She didn't know why she'd put on the black dress, but when she saw it hiding in the back of her closet, she grabbed it.

She never dressed up. This wasn't the first time he'd cooked for her. She'd even cooked for him on occasion. They were always causal. This time she was changing it up. Trying to impress him.

Trying to entice him.

Something. Anything to move things to another level.

"Girl, you look smoking hot. You won't even get to the meal." Ivy smirked like the devil. "And it's about time."

Jo didn't even want to know how Ivy knew they hadn't slept together yet. "Have a good night, Ivy."

"Yep. You too. Do everything that I would do!"

Jo laughed as she left.

She made it to Jason's apartment a short time later. He buzzed her up. Her phone rang right before she would've walked into the elevator.

The caller ID had her stopping before she entered. She couldn't afford to lose signal in the elevator.

"Jake. How are you?"

He hadn't called or returned her calls in the last four months. Not once. So to see his name pop up on her phone now, she couldn't ignore it.

Damn.

Jason would dump her ass soon. She hated canceling on him so much. And if Jake wanted to talk all evening, she would. She'd drop everything for him.

"It's Blake."

Oh no. Jake's brother. Calling from Jake's phone.

"What happened? Is he okay?"

"He's—oh my gosh, Jo. I have no idea why I called you. I shouldn't have bothered you with this problem. I'm so sorry. What was I thinking?"

"Blake, you're not bothering me. Tell me what's going on."

"He's a mess. A complete mess. I should've come sooner. I am so sorry you've called him every day the last four months and he's never answered."

She was too.

There had been a point when she thought about stopping, and yet, every morning, she found herself hitting dial and leaving another message she knew would go unanswered.

"I get it."

"You shouldn't have to get it, Jo. It's not right."

Maybe it wasn't, but she still got it no matter what Blake thought. Jake had to get through this on his own, or at least, she had thought so. Just like she'd done it on her own as well.

Though, ignoring her grief wasn't doing anything. She was embarrassed to admit that while she'd called every day, she hadn't acknowledged what happened in any other way. Perhaps if she had, she would've done more than call Jake. Like his brother had.

They were both failing at managing their grief.

"How can I help?" It was time to change that.

"Help? Oh, God, Jo, I didn't call to get you involved in his problems. I wanted to apologize about his behavior."

But his problems were her problems.

"I'll let you go. I'm so sorry, Jo. I'm so sorry."

Then Blake hung up before she could argue. Not that she had much fight in her right now.

She walked in a trance to Jason's apartment. He opened the door before she could finish the first knock.

"What happened? I knew something was wrong when it

took you too long to get up here. You have to leave, don't you?"

The sadness in his eyes at the prospect hit her hard. She didn't want to leave. She wanted to rewind to before the phone call and pretend none of it happened.

But she couldn't.

Tears burst out of her.

Jason flinched, startled by them. She was a bit shocked herself. She hadn't cried this much since her brother's funeral. And only the one day. The moment she walked out of the cemetery, she'd never cried again.

Warm arms wrapped around her, pulling her inside the apartment. Then she found herself on the couch, cocooned in his embrace. He rubbed his hand on her back, letting her get it all out.

She cried until her head hurt. Even after the tears subsided, neither said a word. Jason held her quietly in his arms, and she let him.

"You look nice tonight. I'm sorry I ruined it."

He'd dressed up, just as she had. They'd been on the same page. Now it didn't matter. Nothing would happen tonight. Nothing could.

Because Jason had been right. She needed to leave.

"You didn't ruin anything. I have to say you look spectacular in this dress."

She sat up and removed herself from his lap. She even got to her feet. Having the conversation she was about to have would be better with distance between them.

Jason stood up as well. She could see the acknowledgement in his eyes. He knew she was leaving.

"I have to go."

"Of course."

This was the first time she hated how understanding he

could be. She didn't know what she wanted, but she didn't want him to acquiesce so easily.

"I'll be gone a while."

He frowned.

She waited for him to dig further. Or maybe he wouldn't.

"I'm..." His lips twisted in unease. "I'm trying to figure out what that means so I guess I'll ask. Are you breaking up with me? That's assuming we're an actual item, which I like to think we are. I know something upset you." His gaze darted to the couch as if to remind her gently that she'd broken down in front of him. "I'm more than happy to give you the space you need. But I need some clarification here."

Break up with him? Three months wasn't a world record on the longest relationship, but for her, pretty damn close. He gave no signs he wanted to end things either, which meant it would go on even longer.

So no, she wasn't breaking up with him. She liked what they had going on. A lot. She wasn't even sure when their friendship had morphed into more. It just happened. Yet, they had never defined it either.

"No, I..." Those treacherous tears were making their way back up. "I have to leave the state."

She had to go to Jake.

She couldn't ignore it any longer.

OKAY. His heart rate hadn't slowed down yet. Still so many unanswered questions, and he could see she was on the verge of crying again.

Why? He wished she'd spill it already. And he was too afraid to ask point blank. Apparently, he'd lost a lot of his confidence when he'd been stabbed and nearly died. He couldn't even ask the woman he was dating what was wrong.

Most of the fear stemmed from the fact she'd tell him it was none of his business. Sure, they talked about themselves. Growing up and going to school and how they got into the professions they had. He even confessed about his struggles after getting stabbed. Looking over his shoulder more often than he liked. Hating crowds when he never used to have that problem. The slight pain he experienced every now and again in his side. Not that he figured she hadn't noticed. He knew she had noticed, so it hadn't been much of a confession. More like confirming her suspicions. She'd been the one to push him to work out more. To do stretches and work the kinks out. He'd shared a lot of himself with her. Way more than she ever shared of herself. He knew there was a lot about her he still didn't know. He never pried because he didn't want to ruin the good thing going between them.

Error on his part. Clearly.

"Whatever you need, Victoria. I'm here for you."

That was all he could offer. He didn't know how to tread these dangerous waters. He felt like he was on a sinking boat. If more water got in, he'd be a goner.

She blew out a breath. "Will you come with me?" Then her eyes slammed shut and she shook her head. "Never mind."

He moved closer, brushing her cheek. She leaned into it but didn't open her eyes. "Of course I will. You don't have to face whatever you're dealing with alone. I'm here for you."

Her eyes gradually opened. "I told you I had a brother." She grabbed his hand, removing it from her cheek and bringing it down to their side. Thankfully, she didn't let go of it. "That he died."

He remembered her sharing the basics. Her brother had died about five months ago. The pain was still very fresh. He hadn't pried because he also sensed it was a sensitive topic. She had never offered the way he'd died.

She'd grown up between Minnesota and New York. Her parents had been divorced, shuffling her and her brother back and forth all the time. She'd stayed in Minnesota after high school, joining the police department with her brother. Two years ago, she moved back to New York. That was the gist of everything she had told him. Now he was on the precipice of learning more. By the tears gathering in her eyes, he wasn't sure he wanted to know more.

"He was killed in the line of duty."

He squeezed her hand. "I'm so sorry, Victoria."

He could only imagine how that must've felt. Junelle worried about Rider every day he left the house. Jason understood why. It was a dangerous profession. He'd never admit it to Victoria, but he worried about her the same way. Hell, he never even mentioned his feelings to Junelle and they were pretty damn close for brother and sister. But he knew Junelle knew he worried as well. How could anyone's significant other not worry about their loved ones when they had such a dangerous profession?

"It's a little more complicated than what you might be thinking. I..." She blew out another breath, the tears escaping.

He guided her to sit down, pulling her into his arms once again. "You don't have to talk about it. It's okay."

She placed a hand on his chest, pushing until she could see his face. "Maybe it's time I tell you. You might not want to join me."

He doubted that. If she needed company for wherever she had to go, he'd be there for her. "I would hope by now you know the kind of guy I am. If you need help, I am here to help you."

Hell, he'd been arrested three times in his life trying to help random women he didn't even know. Of course, he'd be there for his girlfriend.

She swiped her cheeks. "Okay. I'll give you the quick version. My brother worked in the homicide division. It's a hard job. I mean, no job in the department is easy. His partner was Jake Anders. I went through the academy with both of them. Jake's like a brother to me too. Great guy. Solid guy. One of the best."

Okay, he got it. Jake was awesome. Good for him.

He hated how jealousy wormed its way inside his heart. Despite not wanting to hear more praise about Jake, he didn't interrupt. This was too important for her to get out.

"I don't know what happened. I don't know what my brother was thinking. The job is hard. I know this. Maybe he couldn't take it anymore. He was married. Charlotte was nice. I didn't have a problem with her in the beginning. We weren't close or anything. She found me odd like everyone else. Then I hated her because she cheated on my brother. He was also working a pretty horrible case involving the death of a four-year-old. Mom claimed it was an accident. That she left him in the bathtub for just a few minutes to take a phone call. But my brother—even Jake—thought she'd killed him. A little boy. An innocent little boy.

"My brother called Jake one night to get to his house. Though he hadn't been staying there as Charlotte had kicked him out. Which was insane to me because she had been the one cheating! But whatever. After my brother called Jake, the police were called because shots were fired. A neighbor called nine-one-one. Jake got there at the same time, telling everyone to stand down, that he'd check it out.

My brother had shot his wife and her lover, who happened to be there at the time. He also confessed to killing the mother who was suspected of killing her little boy. I never got the full story. I'm not even sure they know the full story with what happened that night. But Jake went inside by himself to assess the situation."

Jason waited with bated breath. Whatever it was would be bad. It had to be. Her brother was dead.

"Jake killed my brother."

The same Jake who was one of the best? Great guy? Solid guy? How was that man any of those things if he killed her brother?

"Anyway, there you have it. The whole story. Jake's brother called me tonight, and I think Jake needs me. I need to go to Minnesota. That's where I'm going. And after hearing all that, you won't want to go with me."

Oh hell no! He had to go with her now. To keep her safe from this Jake guy.

"I'm going with you."

A heavy sigh left her body, as if she'd been holding her breath, waiting for his rejection. "Are you sure?"

"Victoria." He cupped her cheeks so she couldn't look away from him. "What you told me was horrible, and I'm so sorry you had to go through all of that. I sense you've been going through it all by yourself. You don't have to do that anymore. I'm here for you. I'm not letting you go there alone."

What happened was horrific. To think it only occurred five months ago. She didn't act like someone who'd recently lost a sibling in such a violent way. Not even Rider, or any other co-worker, must know what happened. Rider would've shared it with him.

Why would she keep such a secret to herself?

Why would she think she had to grieve on her own? Process such a terrible tragedy all by herself?

Her features crumbled and more tears came out. He pressed her head to his chest, letting her get it all out.

"You can't be real, Jason. No man is this perfect."

He gave a short laugh. "I'm far from perfect."

Her arms wound around him, holding on tight. "I've tried calling him every day since the funeral. He never answers."

This could be where the imperfections came out. Because what he wanted to say about a guy he'd never met was not pleasant. That asshole didn't deserve someone so sweet and kind in his life. Especially one who killed her brother.

Jason had a feeling this was the first time she released her emotions about what happened. She'd been bottling this all inside for way too long.

She lifted her head. "You tensed. What is it?"

Of course she'd feel the rage hit his body. If he was going to go along on this trip, he couldn't lie to her. She'd eventually see how he felt. "I'm not sure Jake deserves such kindness from you."

"No, Jason. You don't understand. He didn't mean to kill Wally, my brother. I know he had no choice. I know it."

"I'm not sure I'd be as forgiving as you if someone killed Junelle. Even if she did commit such unspeakable crimes."

"There's nothing to forgive. Jake was put in an impossible situation. I can't blame him for anything my brother did. It's not his fault. Wally killed three people. I still can't wrap my head around that sometimes. That my brother would do something so heinous. I think that's why I cried so much right now. I've never stopped to think about all of it. If I ignored it, it didn't really happen. Jake's doing the same thing. He's ignoring everything. Everyone. I can't let him do that anymore. I can't let him think he did something wrong. Knowing my brother, he forced Jake to do what he did. He didn't have the guts to do it himself. Because he knew he wouldn't get away with anything he did. And he also knew he couldn't spend his life behind bars."

Well, when she put it that way, it did make some sense. He'd keep his reservations to himself until he met the guy. Then he'd make up his mind whether she should hate him or not.

"When do you want to leave?"

"As soon as possible."

He pressed a light kiss to her lips. "Then let's see if they have a red eye flight."

8

"Sorry I couldn't be more helpful, man."

He chuckled despite the irritation brewing like a storm in the pit of his stomach. "No worries. I get it. Thanks though."

He inclined his head in goodbye and turned to leave. Even took three steps away before Jerry spoke.

"Are you and Tina coming over later tonight?"

The smile plastered on his face said he couldn't wait to have dinner with this moron and his sister. But bringing his girlfriend around him? No. That wasn't going to happen. He didn't share with anyone.

"I can't. Not tonight. Another time. Have a good one, Jerry."

Then he walked faster so the guy couldn't stop him again.

He wasn't sure what to think when his sister told him she had started dating a cop. With the sketch up with his likeness, it had been a risky move to even meet the guy. But he did. They had the double date, and it went well. Tina, the woman his sister hooked him up with, was delightful.

She was also a kindergarten teacher and worked at the same school as May. She was pretty, in a safe, I-would-never-disobey-you way. And she didn't. If he asked for something, she delivered. She wanted to please him in any way she could. It hadn't taken long to get her wrapped around his finger. It'd been a while since he had a girlfriend. She would do for the time being.

He couldn't complain about the sex. The woman might wear lame floral clothes and teach a bunch of obnoxious children—had the patience of a saint—but when it came to the bedroom—diabolical vixen. She loved to try it all.

That had been the deciding factor for him to continue seeing her. The sex was too good to walk away from.

Who knew a prim and proper kindergarten teacher had such a sexual desire hidden under all that sweetness? He sure in the hell had been surprised.

The last three months had been better than expected.

His sister's stupid boyfriend didn't connect the dots he was the same man whose sketch was hanging up on the wall, ten feet from where he worked. The idiot couldn't call himself a real cop. He manned the front desk. A secretary. That's what he was. Nothing more. A real cop would've noticed who he truly was.

He had a girlfriend who was attentive to his needs and delivered the most amazing sex he'd had in a long time.

And Detective Johansen, the blonde bitch working the case, was clueless. She had no idea how to find him. Of course, he made sure of that. Leaving evidence behind was for amateurs. He never left a trace, including his DNA, fingerprints, or face in any camera frame.

So yeah, he couldn't complain about anything the last three months.

Except for the fact he could feel the need growing inside

him again. The aching urge to find a new prey. To stalk them. To take what was rightfully his—all the pleasure.

Sure, Tina satisfied him very well. No complaints in that department.

But she couldn't give him everything he needed. And what he needed was to get rid of the ache filling him up. Gnawing at his gut like a scavenger to a corpse.

Yes. It was time to get back online in the dating game. Find the next woman who would relieve the pain he suffered from.

Once done, he'd be good.

Tina would get his full attention.

He was enjoying his time with her. Though they hadn't been dating long, he could see a future with her. That was a first. He'd never imagined a future with one woman.

Maybe after he created a new online profile tonight, he'd do a little ring shopping.

Then he'd surprise her with a visit and get laid. He was feeling like some rough sex tonight. His Tina would oblige him.

Because she was a good girlfriend like that.

"You okay?"

Jason slid his hand into hers. She was grateful for his support and his willingness to tag along on this depressing trip, but she didn't know how many more times she could handle being asked if she was okay.

No!

She wasn't okay.

They were standing in front of a house where she'd have

to enter and face her demons. Not that she blamed Jake for anything. Not once had she held any sort of hatred or resentment toward him. But that didn't mean it would be easy facing him.

The last time she'd seen Jake had been a few months before everything happened. She'd been in town visiting her brother, so of course that included seeing Jake as well.

Then her brother died.

Everything went to hell.

Jake never showed up to the funeral. And back then she didn't have the guts to reach out to him. It took her a month to even call him. Once she had called him, she'd made sure to do it every day.

"Victoria?" He squeezed her hand.

Either it was his soft-spoken voice or the jolt of his touch, but something snapped her out of her musings.

"I'm fine. Let's go."

What person ever answered, no they weren't okay? Especially when the one asking knew for a fact they weren't. She lied. Jason knew she lied. Yet, he let it go and followed her to the front door.

Before she could knock, the door swung open. Blake, Jake's brother, stood in the threshold. His eyes were hooded with dark circles. He looked sleep deprived, yet his clothes and hair said he took the time to look presentable. No wrinkles present. Hair immaculate as always. Blake didn't do the rough-and-tumble look, so witnessing the dark circles threw her off.

"I saw you standing outside. If you didn't plan on coming onto the porch, I was going to let you leave. You didn't have to come, Jo." Blake's bottom lip trembled as if on the verge of tears.

Happy ones, that she came?

Sad ones, because it was a losing battle they were about to face?

"I should've come sooner. I'm sorry, Blake."

He swore under his breath as he shook his head. "I never want to hear you apologize to me again. You owe Jake nothing. And he owes you everything."

An explanation would be nice about what happened that night. But she wouldn't demand it of Jake. But she could see she and Blake would not agree on the matter. No one needed to understand her feelings about the situation but herself. At times, she didn't even understand her own feelings.

Jo cleared her throat, flashed a phony smile, and gestured at Jason. "This is Jason, my..." Well, her boyfriend. Right?

Why was she hesitating? She had no idea. They'd been together for three months. Yet, their relationship wasn't normal. Especially with the amount of times she left him in the middle of a date. Who wanted to date someone like that? She sure in the hell wouldn't.

"Boyfriend. I'm her boyfriend." Jason held out his hand toward Blake. "It's nice to meet you. I'd like to say up front that I'm not sure I feel the same toward your brother. Victoria knows how I feel. We don't agree on a few things and that's okay. I don't expect her to agree with everything I say or think or feel. I can't know how she feels about this situation. But I'm letting you know how I feel. I'm glad you see Jake as the problem too."

"Jason," she hissed.

His hand tensed, and she felt the vibrating jolt all the way to her stomach.

"Jake is not the problem. I already told you—"

"Victoria, I don't want to argue." Jason shifted his stance so he could look at her. She wanted to avoid his gaze but didn't. "I know what you said back at my apartment. While I see your side of it, it's hard to look away from the fact he killed your brother. That he hasn't given you a reason why. You've struggled the entire trip here. You stood on the sidewalk for over ten minutes staring at the house." Jason thrust a hand toward the said area, his agitation rising. "You tell me you're okay, and we both know you're not. I'm not going to stand in front of this man and pretend like it's all okay. It's not!"

It pained her to do it, but she yanked her hand out of his. "I think I'll go inside by myself right now. I can't do this with you, Jason. We'll agree to disagree."

Then she shuffled past Blake without another comment. To her huge relief, Blake closed the door without allowing Jason to enter.

He'd been so supportive the entire way here. From packing up their belongings to getting the plane tickets to the semi-short drive from the airport to Jake's house.

This was the first time Jason let his feelings be known. She wasn't sure how to take it.

"So Jason seems nice."

She swiveled around, unsure if Blake was being serious or not. His expression wasn't one of jesting.

"He's not wrong either. Jake has some explaining to do and he's not doing it. You deserve that."

"I don't want to do this with you either, Blake. Where is Jake?"

Blake flicked a hand toward the hallway that led to the bedrooms. Jake had a nice, two-bedroom house in a quiet neighborhood. Jo knew the house like the back of her hand.

Which meant she'd find him in the last bedroom on the right.

"Last time I went in there, he wouldn't listen to me, and when I walked out, he locked the door. Good luck, Jo. Maybe he'll be more receptive to you than he is to me."

She hoped so too. Otherwise this would have been a wasted trip. Not that she'd thought Jason would say it out loud, but he'd think 'I told you so' when Jake refused to speak to her.

The trek down the hallway didn't take long and she wished it had. The moment was upon her. Seeing Jake for the first time since her brother died.

She tried the doorknob first, not surprised it was locked. A light tap on the door echoed down the hallway. The house was way too silent for her tastes.

"Jake. It's me, Jo. Can I come in?" She waited a few seconds before adding, "Please."

Nothing but silence answered her.

"Did you know lemons can float, but limes sink in water?" She held her breath for a moment, then released it in a long, hard blow.

Always dropping into her crutch. Her stupid random facts.

Because her nerves were wired so high, she felt like she was going to pass out.

"I find it so hard to believe, I've been meaning to try it out. I haven't yet."

Silence remained.

"Have you ever realized the letter A doesn't appear in any number until one thousand? That one seems impossible as well. I counted to a thousand once to verify the fact."

It had taken her forever too, saying the number and spelling it out in her head as she did so.

Commence continued rambling.

Jason popped his head up and turned his attention toward the front door. Blake stepped outside, shut the door, and took the empty seat next to him. The porch chairs were pretty comfortable. Not that he would've complained if they weren't. But since he was delegated to the outside of the situation, at least he was comfortable where he was at.

"I forgot Jo's first name is Victoria. I've never heard anyone call her that."

Okay. So they were going with idle conversation. Jason could work with that.

"That's how she introduced herself to me. It's impossible to see her as Jo."

Blake settled into his chair. Maybe he found them as comfortable as he did.

"How did you two meet?"

Did he care? Or he didn't want to sit in silence? If that were the case, he hadn't needed to come outside to begin with.

"My sister married one of the detectives she works with. She came to the wedding. She didn't stay the entire time, and when I asked her to dance, she declined. Then a few months ago, she arrested me for rape."

Blake flinched and sat up straighter.

That got the guy's attention.

Jason chuckled, despite nothing being funny.

"I didn't do anything wrong. I stumbled into the situation, since the guy was hurting the woman on my job's premises. He ended up coming back and killing the woman the next day. Or the day after that. I can't remember now.

But I failed that woman when I thought I was helping her." Jason shoved his hands into his face, groaning. "I feel like I'm failing Victoria."

He straightened, snapping his gaze at Blake. "She couldn't even call me her boyfriend. Maybe these past three months I've been deluding myself about what we are. I didn't learn about any of this until last night. The entire morning since we left my apartment has been tense. I shouldn't have come. I don't think she wants me here."

That was abundantly clear.

She didn't even let him accompany her inside the house.

And why the hell was he dumping all his personal issues on this guy? He didn't even know him.

"I don't know where to start. But I will say, if Jo didn't want you here, you wouldn't be here. Nobody makes that woman do anything."

He made a good point.

Then why didn't he feel welcome?

"Thanks for coming even when you don't like my brother."

"I came for Victoria."

Blake nodded, and then silence reigned.

They sat there, a light cool breeze blowing around them. For the end of June, in Minnesota, it was a lot hotter than he anticipated it would be, but the wind helped cool it down.

Jason had no idea how much time passed before the front door opened. Victoria stepped out, agitation written all over her body. It didn't take a rocket scientist to know it didn't go well with Jake.

"The door's still locked."

Blake stood up at Victoria's comment. "I'm sorry he wasn't responding to you either."

"I'm going to take a walk." Then she stepped off the porch without even glancing his way.

He let her go because he wasn't about to cause more friction between them. She needed space and he wanted to give her as much as she needed.

Blake turned his way. "Do you two want to stay for supper? I can throw some steaks on the grill. My wife's here too, but visiting friends right now. She has a hard time being around Jake. She wants to slap some sense into him, but that isn't the way to approach the situation." Blake shook his head, laughing. "And I info-dumped on you. Sorry. Would you like to stay for supper?"

He would prefer not to. If he had his way, they'd catch the first flight out of here.

Instead, he shrugged. "Whatever Victoria wants to do."

"Yeah, that makes sense."

Blake turned to leave.

"Do you have any bobby pins or even the teeny tiny screwdrivers?"

The slow turn and odd expression on Blake's face nearly made him laugh again. "Why?"

"I'm going to pick a lock."

A mischievous grin formed on Blake's face. "I have what you need."

He followed Blake inside. After the man searched a purse for the longest time, he produced two bobby pins.

"My wife's purse."

As if he needed an explanation of whose purse it was. Jason had figured it had been a woman's purse. But hey, if it would've been his, he wouldn't have commented about it. He didn't care if a guy carried a purse around.

Blake pointed down the hallway and told him what door was Jake's. Jason bee-lined it there and got to work. It didn't take more than two minutes to hear the tiny click of the lock disengaging. He twisted the doorknob before Jake could re-lock the door on him.

It shouldn't even have taken him two minutes to do anything. It was a simple doorknob lock where all you had to do was push a tiny device in the right spot to disengage it. A toothpick would've even worked in a pinch. But sometimes it was hard hitting the correct spot.

Jason stepped inside the room. It felt like he'd been swallowed whole in a dark, black pit. The curtains were closed and no lights were illuminated. The bed looked empty, and with the closet wide open, he knew no one was hiding in there. This dude was never going to come out of his depression when he lived like this.

His gaze zoomed to another closed door, presumably the master bathroom.

Was it locked? If so, did he want to tempt fate and pick the lock to such a private area?

A twist of the knob answered the first question. Yep. Locked.

He answered his second question by inserting a bobby pin once again into the tiny hole of the knob.

Maybe he should've knocked and announced himself first, but why? This asshole was causing Victoria pain and suffering, and Jason would not allow it.

The guy wanted to hide away from the world. Fine. He'd let him. As soon as Victoria had her say. Jason would *not* let him continue to ignore her. She deserved whatever answers she demanded of him.

It took him less than a minute this time to unlock the door. When it swung open, the room was as dark as the bedroom.

But he saw the lone figure huddled in the bathtub.

The weapon lying on the edge of the tub with his fingers wrapped around the handle made Jason stay planted in his spot.

Was he about to get shot? Or was the dude about to shoot himself? Either answer was plausible.

He should've knocked first.

Maybe picking the locks of a guy's house who had no problem killing a good friend wasn't the wisest move.

Jake stared at him. Jason could do nothing but return the hard glare back.

At least he wasn't making a move to pick up the weapon, though his fingers were still curled around it, ready for anything.

"You don't know me, but I'm Victoria's boyfriend. Victoria's here. She'd like to speak to you. The least you could do is give her that courtesy."

His soft voice boomed loudly in the dark, small space.

But his words had an effect on Jake because he averted his gaze, shuffling it toward the bottom of the bathtub.

"She told me she calls you every day. You ignore her every day. She deserves better after what you did."

Jake's jaw clenched, and even in the darkness, Jason saw his knuckles tighten as he gripped the gun harder.

Okay. Still getting through to the guy somewhat. Any reaction was better than none.

"I can't say I like you. If you killed my sibling, I'd hate you. So it goes to show that Victoria is a better person than me. Maybe you had no choice. Maybe you did. Right now, I'm giving you no choice. You're going to get out of that damn bathtub and you're going to speak to Victoria when she gets back, even if I have to drag you out of there." Jason eyed the gun. "And yeah, I can see the gun in your hand. You do have a choice there. You can either shoot me or let me drag your ass out."

When Jake still didn't respond, Jason decided that he had no intention of speaking. Yanking his ass out of the tub it was then.

He took a step forward. Before he took a second step, Jake raised the weapon, pointing it at him.

Okay.

So he might be getting shot today.

9

THE WALK DID nothing to soothe her rattled nerves. If she didn't calm herself down somehow, she'd recite all the random facts she knew. And there was a lot stored in her brain.

Jason and Blake weren't on the porch. She assumed they ventured inside, so she did too without knocking.

She found Blake in the kitchen, staring inside the fridge. He flashed her a short grin when he noticed her presence.

"How was your walk?"

Horrible. But she didn't want to get into that.

"Where's Jason?"

Regret hit her like a freight train.

She'd been incredibly rude to him when he'd been nothing but supportive. Just because he had a differing opinion didn't mean she should've pushed him away like she had.

He left her.

She needed him right now and he left her.

There could be no other explanation, considering the way Blake looked at her with such a forlorn expression.

Blake cleared his throat. "Well, he...thought he'd try speaking to Jake."

What?!

That was a terrible idea.

Jason didn't have any good things to say about Jake. Why would Blake allow him to do that?

And yet...

Maybe he could be the one to get through to him when no one else could.

That was wishful thinking on her part.

"I like him, Jo." Blake's brows pleated. "Though he gave a really odd explanation about you arresting him for rape. That's concerning."

A short chuckle escaped before she could stop it. "A misunderstanding. He was trying to help the woman. We still haven't caught the guy who hurt her." Then killed her. But that was also a topic she didn't want to broach.

Another throat cleared. This time from behind her.

She turned around, her eyes widening in surprise.

Jason stood near the hallway, a gun dangling from his hand. Where did he get a gun from, and why was he holding it?

Jake stood a few feet in front of him.

He looked awful. Hair in disarray, and if she had to guess, he hadn't showered in a few days. He hadn't shaved in a long time, with the beard covering his entire jaw line and cheeks. She'd never seen Jake in a beard. His clothes were wrinkled and his whole body was rigid. As if Jason had forced him to walk out of the room. By gunpoint?

"Hi, Jake."

Nothing but a blank, desolate stare answered.

Coming had been an impulse. An immediate desire to try

and...help Jake somehow. She wasn't even sure. All she knew was when Blake called and informed her of what was going on, she knew she had to be here. Now that she was standing in front of him face-to-face, she didn't know what to do or what to say.

"Why are you here, Jo?"

The despair in Jake's voice nearly made her crumble to the floor. She wanted to wrap him up in a hug and not let go until he released some of his pain.

"Because."

That's the only explanation she could give.

Then Jake walked past her toward the sliding door to the back yard and walked outside, taking a seat at the patio table.

Jason moved closer and set the gun on the counter. "He had this with him in the bathroom. You might want to lock it up somewhere else. Like, away from this house." Then he pushed it closer to Blake.

He retrieved the weapon. "I had no idea he had a weapon in the house. I know they haven't returned his service weapon."

"Is he even working?" Jo asked. She'd be shocked to hear he was, especially with the state of his appearance.

"No. He hasn't been back. He can't return until he sees the department psychologist, and he's refusing to. If I had my way, he'd move to Neptune with me. I think a change of scenery and a change of pace would be good for him."

She'd never been to Neptune, but she knew it was a small, quaint town in northern Minnesota. She had to agree with Blake. A change of scenery would be good for Jake. Something. Anything to get him out of the despair he'd fallen into.

Blake left the room to get rid of the gun.

Jo faced Jason, suddenly afraid of what he might say now that they were alone.

"I'm—"

"He—"

They both smiled, yet no laughter escaped. They had a habit of speaking at the same time.

She waved for him to go first, not quite ready to voice what had been on the tip of her tongue.

"He pointed the gun at me."

She inhaled sharply at the confession, reaching out her hand to comfort him, but stopped short of touching him when he waved her off. It hurt. But she deserved it.

"I've never had a gun pointed at me. It was a completely different feeling from when I got stabbed and it came out of nowhere."

She didn't know what to say, so silence reigned for a beat. But she had to say something.

"How did you get the gun from him?"

A wry smirk punctured his lips. "I asked nicely."

Which she translated into he demanded Jake put it down. Neither looked like they'd gotten into a brawl, so Jake must've surrendered the weapon without a fight. Yet, he'd pointed it at her boyfriend. Someone she cared about. Someone she could picture spending her life with.

Someone she loved.

She moved forward without thinking about it and placed her hand on his heart. He didn't stop her and push it away.

"Did you know the heartbeats of two people in love synchronize?"

Jason's eyes flashed with surprise.

"Studies proved that it's real."

"I've never doubted one of your facts," Jason whispered, as his heart beat a rapid tune.

She placed her free hand over her heart, feeling the same quick pace. Maybe it was her mind playing tricks on her, but they felt in sync with each other.

"I'm sorry, Jason. I don't know why I treated you the way I did earlier. Forgive me, please."

He wrapped his hands around her waist and pulled her closer. She dropped her hands and enveloped him in return. They were chest to chest, and she soaked up every second. Because who knew when it would all come crumbling down. It always did for her.

"I don't want any apology from you, Victoria," he whispered in her ear. "None of this is easy on you and it's okay. I'm sorry for the things I said. For making you feel like I wasn't on your side." He pressed a kiss to her neck. "If I understand what you're saying, then I'll say it too. I love you."

She popped her head up, albeit too fast, knocking into his chin. He groaned in pain, rubbing his jaw, then flashed her a wicked smirk.

"Don't hurt this beautiful head of yours." He caressed the top of her head, brushing her hair away from her cheek. "I never want to see you hurt. My anger got the best of me with how much this whole situation is hurting you."

She rubbed his chin, hoping to soothe the ache she caused. "Oh, Jason, I love you too. I've never been in love before. I didn't think it would come out of nowhere like this. I know we haven't been together long...I don't think I could've done this without you. I don't think I can face Jake without you. I knew this would be hard, but I didn't realize how hard. My point is, thank you for being here. Thank you for being honest. And thank you for doing the hard parts I can't seem to do."

"That's where you're wrong. You can do anything you set your mind to, no matter how hard it is. I haven't done anything here." Jason twisted his head to look out the large bay window. "It might seem like I forced him out here, but I doubt that man can be forced to do anything. He walked out here because he knows he has to face you sooner or later."

He kissed her on the lips, holding the sweet touch for a few seconds longer than he normally did.

"Blake invited us for supper. Do you want to stay?"

No, she wanted to run as far away from this situation as possible.

Instead, she gave a quick nod.

Because sometimes a person had to do things they didn't want to.

He didn't want to face Jake again, especially so soon. How did one get past the fact a gun was pointed at your face? He was still reeling from it.

Imminent death.

So different from the surprise attack. He had time to process he might get shot. Time to let his life flash before his eyes.

When he'd been stabbed, it came out of nowhere. There wasn't any moment for him to have regrets or think about the good memories. Nothing but pain surfaced, and then nothing but blackness because he'd passed out from the blood loss.

But he couldn't let Victoria walk outside and confront

Jake by herself. He knew she wasn't ready for that, even if she was pretending like she was.

She stepped outside onto the back deck first with him hot on her tail. They took a seat at the table, across from Jake.

"I wish you wouldn't have come, Jo."

There was no inflection in Jake's tone of voice. Now that he understood the guy a little better, Jason wasn't surprised.

"And I wish you'd talk to me. I guess we all can't get what we want."

Jake's eyes flared with life, an emotion Jason couldn't quite name. Because as fast as it appeared, it vanished.

If they kept persisting, eventually they'd get through to him.

Except no one spoke. The wind blew sporadically, offering brief moments of coolness. Jason would've loved a nice, cold drink, but he'd be damned if he got up and left Victoria alone.

Minutes passed.

The silence stretched.

The heat made the sweat roll down his back.

The wind, despite its presence, didn't do enough to reduce the heat spreading around the area. Not just from the high temps. If someone lit a match, they'd all burst into flames.

"Let me go get us all some lemonade." Then Victoria shoved back her chair and raced into the house.

Jason understood the need to get away from the table. He wished he could too, but this was an opportunity he couldn't pass by.

"Stop being an asshole to the kindest woman I've ever met. She doesn't deserve your attitude."

Jake's gaze moved away from the deck toward him.

Nothing stared back at him. No anger. No sadness. Complete emptiness in the dark depth of his eyes. Jason wasn't surprised by that either.

"I don't even know who you are. So don't tell me what to do."

"Victoria's boyfriend. I told you that. Jason Swanson. My sister married my best friend, Rider, who also works with Victoria. Now you know me. Stop being a damn asshole."

Jake stared at him for the longest time, his eyes filled with varying emotions. "I don't know what she wants from me." Jake sighed so hard, it's as if part of his soul left his body. "Except for her brother back. I can't give her that."

"How about an explanation about what happened that night. Maybe that's what you both need to move on."

A strangled laugh left Jake's lips. "You think I have a chance of moving on? In what deranged world do you live in? I killed my best friend. There's no moving past that."

He had a point. Wrong choice of words.

"Okay, moving on wasn't the best way to describe it. How about to continue living. Because right now," Jason waved his hand up and down, "this isn't living. What you're doing is getting by. That's no way to live."

Jake tore his gaze away, looking into the backyard. It was a small yard, fenced in. The wooden fence was high enough to give plenty of privacy from the neighbors. They were cocooned in a tiny space, away from prying eyes. Hopefully ears too.

"Do you want to know what kills me the most?" Jake whispered, his words nearly swept away by the strong gust of wind. It made Jason doubt what he'd heard. Until Jake continued. "That I didn't see my best friend was struggling. I didn't see he'd hit his limit on what he could handle. I mean, it's one thing to kill your wife and lover, the rage boiling over the top. I don't condone it, but I get why he did it. But it was him killing that mother who'd killed her child. That I couldn't comprehend. We had suspicions, but not actual concrete evidence."

Jake lowered his head, his chin almost resting on his chest. His voice lowered even more. "I told him it was okay. That the mother deserved it. I actually said that to him. I thought he'd put the gun down. I thought if I appealed to his emotions in such a way, he'd listen to me."

Jason held his breath, afraid to even make the slightest sound. He doubted Jake had spoken like this to anyone yet.

Why him?

Why now?

How did he respond to any of it?

"When he pointed the gun at me, he said..." Jake lifted his head, the agony pouring from his eyes. Not the unknown emotion he saw earlier. This one wasn't hard to decipher. "What did you think when you had a gun pointed at you?"

He flinched, caught off guard by the question. Then he blurted out the first thing that came to mind.

"I thought about my sister and how much I love her. I thought about Victoria and how I didn't do the things I wanted to do with her, to say to her. I thought about my best friend Rider and how much time I wasted being away from him when he walked away from me for five damn years. I thought..." Shit. Sharing feelings was hard. But at the moment, necessary. Someone had to get through to Jake, and apparently he got hired for the job. "I thought it would've been nicer if you'd pulled the trigger right away instead of letting me think so many damn thoughts. Because not knowing what's coming is far better than seeing it happen in slow motion."

Another long stare from Jake held him captivated.

"I was stabbed a year ago. Came out of nowhere. I felt nothing but pain. For the longest time since it happened, I've been afraid of everything, even my own damn shadow. I realize now, since you pointed a gun at my face, I can't be afraid of what might happen. I don't want to be afraid of what might happen. If it happens, it happens. I didn't like having that warning. So if you plan on shooting me in the future, just do it."

That garnered a short chuckle out of Jake. It sounded foreign coming from him, as if he'd never laughed in his life.

"Duly noted." Jake ran a ragged hand through his hair, another sigh emanating in the air. "His hand didn't shake or tremble in the slightest as he held the gun in my face. He said, 'I don't want to shoot you, Jake, but I will. Don't make me do it. So you know what you have to do.'"

A ragged sound escaped. Jason wasn't sure if it was another laugh or a strangled cry.

"He'd killed three people. His wife, who I knew he still loved despite the fact she cheated on him. He wasn't lying saying he'd shoot. He'd proved that with his actions. He fired his weapon first."

Jason sat up straighter. Victoria never mentioned Jake had been shot in the incident.

"And at the sound of it, I returned fire. Mine hit him in the chest. His shot went wide, embedding in the wall behind me. Though I swore I heard it buzz past my ear. My best friend made me kill him and I hate him for that. I can get over everything else he did, but I can't seem to forgive that." Jake's expression hardened into a fierce frown that bordered on fury and despair rolled into one. "So how in the hell do you expect me to believe Jo can forgive me?"

"Because, even though you haven't shared any of this with her, she knows what happened inside that house. She already believes Wally gave you no choice." Jason leaned closer. "And because she has such a sweet, giving heart, she doesn't know how not to forgive. It's in her nature to see the good in everything."

Jake's stormy mood evaporated. "I'm sorry for pointing a gun at you. I was never going to shoot."

"Yeah, well, you're not getting it back anytime soon. Not until you get your head out of your ass."

Another tiny laugh slipped out, floating away with the wind. "I don't know if I can talk to Jo like I did with you."

"Then don't. But stop pushing her away. You owe her that much."

Jake met his gaze. "How did you two meet?"

"Well, it's an interesting story."

And not a flattering one. At least, not when he described it to Blake.

"Considering I've never liked any guy Jo's dated before, I'm willing to give you a chance to convince me why I should like you. I like interesting stories."

Despite not thinking it would ever happen, Jason was starting to like Jake. The guy wasn't so bad...once a person got past the tough exterior.

"Okay. We first met at my best friend's wedding. Not a great interaction. Then the next meeting, she arrested me..."

10

His mood had been excellent since last night. He was still reeling from the high. Because a beautiful woman was about to get lucky. Not just any woman either. The best kind.

The one the stupid woman detective would never see coming.

He had a date lined up.

It wasn't until next week, but that was okay. It would give him time to do his research. To observe. To find out every tiny detail he'd need to succeed.

When he went on the hunt, details were crucial in success. If one little piece was off, it spelled trouble.

Like what happened with his last date. Getting interrupted in the act had not been planned. He'd watched that construction site for two weeks before deciding it was time. No one had been there after five o'clock.

Damn asshole had messed it all up.

Though, he enjoyed taking the woman twice. Letting her feel a bit of freedom, only to take it all away.

And the stupid cops. His picture—the semi-near sketch

—hung up on the wall. He passed by it every time he was in the precinct. It made him want to laugh each time he saw it.

"Hey, appreciate your time, Detective Roco."

Now he could enjoy walking past his picture, chuckling to himself. His job for the day was done. Though, he'd never laugh out loud. That would draw attention, and he would never do something so risky.

"Yeah, anytime. See ya later."

He nodded with a smile and turned around. The precinct, as usual, was bursting with energy. Loud and in-your-face. He liked it that way. It stopped people from noticing things in their surroundings that they should've otherwise been aware of.

"Hey. Hold up."

He paused in his leisure strides, twisting around toward the one voice he tried to avoid. Detective Tate Powell grated on his nerves.

"Detective Powell, hello." Then he turned his gaze toward the man's partner, smiling even wider. "And Detective Stromberg. Is there something I can help you with?"

"You're working the Anderson case? Yeah?" Powell asked.

What the hell was it to him? Despite wanting to rip his head off for daring to ask him such a question and butting in his business, his smile remained.

"It's one of them, yes. I work on many cases."

"Well, make sure you do your job correctly. You have a tendency of stretching the facts."

The audacity of this man...

To question his integrity.

He worked every case with the utmost care, gathering information and presenting it with accurate facts. To suggest he'd embellish or misconstrue any of his cases more than grated on his nerves. It sent his fury skyrocketing.

"I don't recall asking for your opinion."

Powell's eyes narrowed. "Well, you're getting it. That little girl—"

Stromberg cleared his throat. "We're giving you a friendly reminder."

"I don't need your friendly reminder. I take offense to anything you're suggesting right now."

Powell stepped closer. "I don't give a shit. You were wrong about the Hoffman case. So if you think you're going to blast the little Anderson girl the same way, you're wrong."

Ah, the Hoffmans. Yes, they had been an interesting case. Husband worked on Wall Street. Wife stayed at home —with no kids. A trophy wife. A woman with no brains. Though she had a beautiful body, so he could see why the guy had married her. He imagined she'd been amazing in bed. They'd been shot in their home. A robbery gone bad, the lead detective had predicted.

He'd thought otherwise.

Because he did his job, unlike some cops. The husband had been cheating on his wife. The wife had been cheating on her husband. So no, not a robbery gone bad. More like a marriage that had fallen apart. The lovers had done it. Together.

He knew because he'd followed them. Overheard them speaking about it.

That was thing about him. He could blend in a crowd. He could slink in a corner. No one knew he was around.

Not his fault the lead detective couldn't figure it out.

Not surprising.

They couldn't figure out he'd killed anyone either.

"Are you threatening me, Detective Powell?"

Powell's lips twisted in a devilish manner. "I never threaten. I make promises. You'd do well to remember that."

"Sure. No problem. Have a wonderful day, detectives."

Then he turned around, done with the conversation.

No one told him what to do.

He was about to show all of them what he was truly capable of.

"You outdid yourself, Blake. Delicious." Jo meant it. It'd been a while since she had such a wonderful steak from the grill.

She didn't have a grill, and she rarely went out to eat in a restaurant. Takeout was a high occurrence, or quick meals that could be consumed shortly after she got home from work. Sometimes, Jason cooked for them, but it didn't happen often.

She worked too much to let it happen.

"Thanks, Jo. Glad you enjoyed it." Blake stood up, grabbing his plate and a few other items to clear the table.

"I'll help you." Jason stood as well, grabbing more items.

Jo swore he also glared at Jake, giving him a silent message. As if these two were planning all along to give them time to themselves.

They both retreated inside, leaving her alone with Jake.

He hadn't said much all evening. She, Jason, and Blake had held most of the conversation. Talking about mundane stuff. She avoided her job, though did inquire how Blake's company was going. He owned his own carpentry business. He made the most beautiful pieces of furniture on the planet. He and Jason had a lot to talk about, seeing as Jason owned a construction company. Almost the same thing.

They both built things with their hands.

"I like Jason."

She flinched at the sound of Jake's voice, surprised he decided to speak.

"I don't remember a time I've liked one of the guy's you've dated. Quite an interesting way you two met."

A tentative smile brushed across her lips. She hadn't expected this, but she'd go along with it. Because he was speaking to her after months of silence.

"Yeah, what a story to tell our kids. Hey, Mom arrested Dad." Her eyes bulged into round circles. "Not that we're having kids. Or even a future. I mean...did you know that there are four hundred and twenty-one words for snow in the Scottish language?"

A slow, tiny grin built on Jake's face.

The look was so odd because she hadn't seen him smile in ages. She didn't even care it was because he was no doubt laughing at her.

"Why don't you see a future with him?"

This was not a topic she wanted to discuss. Their relationship was so new. Sure, they'd shared the L-word earlier in the day, but did that automatically mean future? As in, forever kind of future?

"Well...did you know—"

Jake held up his hand for her to stop, and she obediently listened. "I'm not trying to make you uncomfortable, Jo. I like your facts, but I don't want you nervous with me." His gaze drifted toward the table. "I'm sorry."

For what? Though she didn't ask.

It could be for a whole host of things.

"I told him I love him. He returned the sentiment." Jake's gaze lifted toward her, so she continued. "I've never been in love. I don't know what to do. I don't want to screw it up."

"You can't screw it up, Jo. Because you're amazing and it's impossible for you to screw things up. I'm sorry about Wally. If you...if you have...questions...I can answer them."

Even though he didn't want to. His hesitation said it all. While she appreciated him bringing it up, now that the moment was upon her, did she want to know it all?

"I...don't have questions."

Jake's brows drew inward, confused.

"I don't need to know what happened inside that house. I can only imagine. You would have never hurt Wally unless it was necessary, so I know he forced you to do it. I don't need to rehash that." She leaned forward, reaching out her hand. "I want my friend back. I don't like seeing you struggle like this, Jake. My brother did what he did and there's no changing that. I don't hold it against you. So stop holding it against yourself."

His movements were slow, but his fingers eventually connected with hers. "I don't deserve your friendship, but I'm going to take it anyway. Thank you, Jo. I'm an asshole. And I'm sorry I treated you like one. I listened to every voice message you left. I hated myself every time I deleted one and didn't call you back. But your voice kept me sane when all I wanted to do was fall apart."

She squeezed his hand. "I'll always be here for you."

He returned the pressure on her hand, then let his slip from her grasp. Apparently, he could handle only so much comfort. "So back to Jason. I like seeing you happy. I'm glad he makes you happy. Take it one day a time. Don't overthink it. Because you know you overthink shit way too much."

His accompanying laughter was hard to resist, so she didn't. She joined in. He wasn't wrong.

Blake and Jason came back outside to find them

laughing and talking as if the night hadn't been stilted an hour ago.

To hear Jake laughing again...she never thought the day would come.

They left an hour later to a hotel not more than a mile from Jake's house.

She needed a shower, though would've preferred a bath. But there was no way she was taking a bath in a hotel room. Weird. The hot water soothed her bones. Somewhat, anyway. But not nearly enough as a bath would've helped.

So many emotions raced through her mind as she stood under the spray. Too many. The tears mingled with the water. Then they turned into sobs.

Jason's voice didn't penetrate right away. It was the sound of the curtain moving that had her looking up into his concerned face. Somehow, she'd found her way to the bottom of the tub, sitting with her arms wrapped around her knees.

"Shit, Victoria, your skin is all red." Jason shut off the water and grabbed a towel from the shelf above the toilet.

The top of her arms were a bit red. She sat under the water for far longer than she realized, the faucet turned as hot as it could go. She'd zoned out. Nothing mattered but releasing all the pain that had been trapped inside.

He wrapped the towel around her shoulders, cocooning her in its warmth. Then he knelt down, brushing wet strands of hair off her face. "I don't want to say the wrong thing here, but what the hell did Jake say to you? I thought...you two were laughing. I thought it was going well. Now I find you crying. Talk to me."

"Jake and I are good. I..." She rested her head on her knees, staring into Jason's loving eyes. "I can't talk about it right now."

Because she didn't know how to explain what she was feeling. Closure, in a way. Sure, Jake didn't go through all the gory details, but he'd confirmed her intuition was correct. Anger at her brother for causing all of this to happen. Sadness because she knew one talk hadn't made Jake magically better and ready to face the world again.

"Then you don't have to."

"I'm fine. I'll be right out. I didn't mean to scare you."

His expression said he didn't believe her, and she didn't blame him. She wasn't fine.

Her legs wobbled as she stood up as soon as Jason left the room. It took longer than usual to dry herself because she felt so weak. Her emotions were spent. She felt empty inside.

In her dazed state, she hadn't thought to bring a change of clothes with her to the bathroom. There was no way she was putting on her old clothes.

Wrapped in the towel, she walked into the main room. Jason's eyes flared to life with the desire she saw anytime they were together. Though, ever the gentlemen, he didn't move toward her. Because he knew now wasn't the right time for that kind of thing.

But when would be the right time?

Maybe what she needed was to lose herself in something else for a while.

The towel dropped to the floor.

This time there was no mistaking the passion blazing in his eyes.

She let him take his fill, then crawled into bed under the covers.

"You're joining me, right?"

"Yes!"

He scrambled out of his clothes so fast, she couldn't hide her smile.

Then he pulled her into his arms, holding her close. Skin to skin. Chest to chest. Heartbeats in sync once again. Both racing like they were heading for the finish line.

Instead of the moment turning passionate, her emotions took another sharp turn. The tears came once again, this time soaking into his warm skin.

"I got you, Victoria. Let it out. It's okay."

With those whispered words, she knew it to be true. It would always be okay with him.

11

Jason blinked a few times, hating the sun penetrating through the tiny slit between the curtains. He hadn't closed them all the way like he thought he had.

His arm tightened around Victoria, then he cursed himself inside his head. The last thing he wanted to do was wake her. She'd had a rough night. First, crying so much she had given herself a massive headache. He had no idea so many tears could come out of one person.

Once they'd stopped, she'd used the bathroom and came right back into his arms. He held her in silence until she'd fallen asleep. But that didn't stop her from tossing and turning all night. Even spoke out loud in her sleep a few times. Mentioning her brother. Saying Jake's name. Nothing but nightmares. He'd felt helpless the whole time. Holding her close hadn't seemed like enough.

They were finally in a bed together—naked—and he felt so out of his depth. How to comfort her. How to make things better. Was he coming on too strong? Not strong enough? Should he have kept his boxers on? Slept on the tiny sofa, if one could even call it a sofa? What the hell did people call those things? It was—

"Jason?"

He froze, his thoughts dashing away. Then he loosened his fingers on her shoulder, unaware he'd tightened his grip.

"Morning." He threw a smile out there, hoping to ease the tension that had risen in the room.

"You had such an intense expression." She swiped a tender hand across his scruffy cheek. "What's wrong?"

You didn't sleep well. I would love to know the nightmares you had. I feel like I'm messing up left and right. I want to help you any way I can.

"Nothing's wrong. The sun woke me. I'm still trying to wake up. I didn't mean to wake you up in the process."

There was no way he would voice what he really wanted to say. It could bring on another round of crying, and he wasn't sure he could handle that. It broke his heart the first time.

She gave him a lazy grin, but he saw the anguish in her eyes. She couldn't hide her true feelings from him. Not when they were so close to each other.

"Thank you."

"For?" He cocked a brow.

"For being you. For letting me cry. For coming with me."

He wrapped his arms around her, kissing the top of her head. "I never need thanks for that. I love you. I would do anything for you."

"I must look a horrible mess. I should take a shower."

"You're beautiful. A few tears won't change that."

Were her eyes red-rimmed and puffy? Yes.

Did she look exhausted to the extreme? Yep.

Was her skin a bit pale? Yeah.

But none of that took her beauty away. If anything, the

way her walls broke down yesterday, letting him in, made her even more gorgeous than before.

She put her hand on his chest as if to use it for leverage to twist away from him, and she did slightly. Half-sitting, she paused, looking back at him.

"Did you just say you love me?"

He lifted himself up and leaned on his elbow. "I told you yesterday that I loved you." Or did he conjure that conversation in his mind? Had he heard her wrong?

She brushed his rough cheek again. God, he needed to shave. He'd dated quite a few women who didn't like to feel bristles on his face, especially when they kissed.

"You said it so casually...I love you too." She giggled. "I've never gone through this before. I don't know how to act. Is that weird?"

"Only if you think me overanalyzing everything I say to you before I say it is weird. Because I don't want to say the wrong thing and mess this up."

Her eyes trailed a path from his face down his chest and to the start of the blanket covering his hips.

Like that, his desire rose. His cock sprung to life. To be fair, it had already been alert and ready for action. But the way she looked at him, hardened it even more.

"We're quite a pair, aren't we?" She elicited another giggle.

"You're damn right we are."

Then he closed the distance between them and kissed her. He didn't even care about morning breath and everything else he should worry about after waking up.

They were naked—in a bed. They had been all night. While last night, this hadn't even been on his mind, not with the way she cried in his arms. There was no ignoring it now.

She moaned in delight, falling into his arms.

They kissed as if they'd never be able to kiss again. With a frenzied need he'd never experienced before.

Hands wove around on both sides. They explored, touching, caressing, and learning every curve before them.

He broke the kiss, breathing heavily. "Victoria..."

"Yes."

Though he hadn't even got out what he wanted to say, she knew what he had been about to voice.

He scrambled out of bed and to his bag, grabbing a condom. Loud crinkles filtered the air along with a low groan as he sheathed himself. There was no damn way he'd last long. Shit!

As soon as he was back in position, Victoria was guiding him to where he belonged. Deep inside.

They both moaned in unison the moment he entered her.

"Give me a moment, sweetheart. Shit!" He bent his head, loving and hating how glorious it felt to be so connected with her. Then he lifted his gaze. "Okay, round one is going to be quick. But I will take my time with round two."

She giggled, pressing her hips up, eliciting another groan from him. "How many condoms did you bring?"

"A whole box. Why?"

She laughed. "Assuming you were going to get lucky, did you?"

It felt like there could be a wrong answer here.

"I assumed nothing."

"Jason." She grabbed his arms, brushing her hands up until she hit his back, then scrapped her nails down until she hit his ass. "What are you waiting for? We can have as many rounds as we want."

And if they ran out of condoms, he'd make a store run.

He pulled out, then thrust back in. Over and over as she

met him each time. He knew it'd be like this with her. Full of wonder and happiness. But the urgency surprised him. They both couldn't stop the fast pace they'd set. Like their heartbeats raced when they touched each other's hearts. As if they didn't rush to the finish line, the game would be over before they won.

"Shit..." He was too damn close. That's what happened when sex wasn't a common occurrence. Especially with a woman he'd been dying to have for over three months. "Victoria!"

Her name roared out of his mouth as his orgasm hit with a ferocity he'd never experienced before. The bliss spread throughout his limbs, relaxing every part of his body. He wanted to drop to the bed, cuddle her close, and go back to sleep.

But they had round two to accomplish.

And damn!

She needed release.

He sat up a bit, touching her where their bodies connected. Her eyes closed as his fingers did their magic. Her hips moved, and as much as he wanted to move his body with her, he resisted. This was about her. Not him. He already felt like a jackass for coming without her.

He leaned down, brushing tiny kisses along her neck, nipping on her ear. "That's it, sweetheart. Come for me. I'm so sorry I didn't wait."

Her nails scratched down his back. "You can make it up to me in round two." Then she screamed his name, the ecstasy spreading across her face as he hit the right spot.

Let round two commence.

"It's nice to see you enjoying the fresh air today." And not holed up in his room like he'd been yesterday when they arrived.

Maybe they were making headway with Jake. He even grinned as she took a seat at the patio table.

"Where's Jason?" Jake stared at her with a critical eye. His perusal made her antsy and nervous.

Did she have something on her face? Other than extreme happiness.

"Inside chatting with Blake. No doubt, this is their way to give us time alone. Blake jumped into a conversation right away and I felt on the outside of it."

His eyes narrowed, staring harder. "You look different this morning." Then a brilliant smile lit up his face. She thought she wouldn't see that kind of look for ages. "You look relaxed."

Talking about her sex life was not something she wanted to do. Did they chat about their significant others and such in the past? Yeah, of course. She had gone to her brother and Jake about most everything. She hadn't been shy about it.

But she never talked about sex. Or asked about their life in the bedroom either. It was one topic off-limits between them.

"I slept..." Horribly. The images she conjured...

She couldn't think about it.

But as soon as she woke up, the morning had been nothing but amazing. They had sex twice in the bed, then showered together. She'd never done something like that before with a guy. It had been more fun than she realized. They'd taken their time exploring each other under the spray. Before they got dressed, they had one more round of sex on the bed.

It's as if they made up for lost time. For the three months of celibacy.

So she might've had a horrible night of sleep, but she'd been rejuvenated by life-altering sex.

"You slept..." Jake laughed. "I lost you, Jo. Where did you go?"

She blinked, coming back to the present. "I had a good morning."

"I can see that." His shit-eating grin didn't even bother her. Because it was wonderful to see such emotion back on his face.

They shared goofy grins, letting silence fill the area. But the longer they remained silent, the more their smiles dimmed.

Fun time was over.

"How long do you plan on staying, Jo?"

She hadn't quite figured that out yet. "Depends. How long are you going to keep hiding from the world?"

He tore his gaze away from her and stared out into the back yard. "Blake asked me the same thing this morning over pancakes. He makes some damn good pancakes. His wife, Mindy, makes them even better."

"I haven't seen her here. Where is she?"

It would be nice to say hello to her, but she also didn't want to know his answer yet about hiding from the world.

Jake shrugged. "I haven't seen her much either, but I know she came here with Blake. I don't think she wants to be around me."

"No..." Jo leaned forward. "Mindy loves you." Jake had welcomed her into the family and treated her like a sister. Vice versa. Jo couldn't imagine Mindy would turn her back on him. Not when Blake supported him as he was.

Jake didn't respond and she didn't know how to continue this line of conversation. Back to her original question.

"What did you tell him? You need to come back to the living world, Jake."

He took his time turning his head back toward her. "He said I should move up to Neptune with him. Get away from the city."

It wasn't a bad idea. Of course, she didn't want to sway him either way. Whatever Jake decided, it had to be up to him.

"Okay. Again, what did you tell him?"

"I'm happy for you, Jo. I love seeing you so happy." Jake looked down at the table. "I don't foresee myself ever getting to that point in my life. Being as happy as you are. Finding love."

Oh, Jake...

She wanted to wrap him up in her arms and squeeze all the love she had for him into his body. Let him absorb it all so he would never say something like that again.

His gaze met hers once again. "And if I stay here, I doubt I'll survive. It pains me to admit that, but it's the truth. I'm going to start packing today and move. I'd like to think this will be a fresh start, but I'm not holding my breath."

"I'll help you pack and move. I like this decision. A fresh start is what you need."

She reached out her hand and waited several long seconds before Jake grabbed a hold of it.

"When I go back to New York, it doesn't mean I'm done with you. It doesn't mean I'm out of your life. No more ignoring me. No more not calling me back. It's time to look to the future and stop dwelling on the past."

"Easier said than done, Jo," he whispered, pain etching across his face. "Every time I close my eyes, I see him. The vacant look in his eyes. The bullet hole in his chest. The blood everywhere. I doubt I'll ever get that out of my head."

Oh, she understood that well. Not that she knew what it looked like, but her nightmares painted a grisly picture.

"I'm here for you, night or day. Don't ever forget that, Jake. Promise me you won't forget that."

He squeezed her hand. "I would never bother you with my—"

She squeezed even harder back. "Promise me!"

Jake swallowed, his Adam's apple bobbing. "Fine. I promise. Expect to hear from me every night then."

"Good. I like chatting with my best guy friend."

Their hands broke apart as Jake chuckled. "Who is your best girl friend? Don't tell me it's Ivy."

Considering she didn't have any other friends—besides co-workers—well, yeah, it was Ivy. Though she'd never use the word 'best' in front of the word friend to Ivy's face. She probably didn't think the same about her.

"Who else would it be? She's crazy sometimes, but I can rely on her, and I can't say that about a lot of people."

"She is crazy. Won't argue with that."

They laughed together again.

Every time the beautiful sound escaped his lips, her heart sang with joy. Slowly but surely, Jake would become the man she remembered him as. Full of life. Willing to help out anyone. A bulldog at his job.

Happy.

"Should probably start packing. I have a lot of shit."

She inhaled a deep breath and let it out in slow increments, raising her face to the sun. "One more minute out here. It's such a beautiful morning and it's not too hot out yet. Let's enjoy this moment."

He dipped his head in acknowledgement but said nothing in return.

Because this was a momentous time. Jake was taking a huge step into forgiving himself. Maybe it hadn't sunk in yet, but it eventually would.

This trip had been impulsive but necessary. Look at all she'd accomplished too.

Getting Jake back on track.

Realizing she loved Jason.

Finally consummating that love.

12

THE APARTMENT DOOR SLAMMED, making him flinch. He hadn't meant to shut it so strongly. No doubt he'd get a complaint from his neighbor, Tasha, across the way. But whatever. Nothing would bring down his mood. Not after the week he had.

When they flew to Minnesota, Jason had no idea how long they'd stay. A whole week hadn't been planned when he left, but he also hadn't been mad about it.

Some days had been tense, filled with a lot of varying emotions. Other days had been light and carefree. It had been an odd combination.

Jake was all moved and in his new location—Neptune. A small town in northern Minnesota. Cute and quaint. Jason enjoyed the few days they spent there. In between unpacking and getting Jake settled, he and Victoria had also done some sightseeing. A bit of hiking on some pretty tough trails. A picnic one day that he tried to make as romantic as he could.

And the last night they'd watched the sunset overlooking one of the lakes in the area. It had been a night to remember.

The trip hadn't just made him and Victoria closer; it brought them together like he'd never been with a woman. So close to each other, he was contemplating looking for rings.

Three months into a relationship!

Ring shopping!

He had to be insane.

So it was a good thing they parted ways at the airport. He needed time to cool down and let them get back into a normal groove. Because nothing that happened in Minnesota had been normal. They'd been thrust into a situation, and emotions were always heightened when that happened.

Now that they were back in the city, back to their daily lives, things would slow down. Their relationship had gone over a tiny hill and he liked that. But he wasn't sure Victoria was ready to jump over a huge mountain. And buying a ring would be like skipping climbing the world's smallest mountain first, Mount Wycheproof, and scaling Mount Everest instead as if he even knew how to climb.

A knock on his door had him swiveling around with his bag still in his hand.

Geez. His neighbor was already going to give him grief for slamming his door.

Except when he opened it, Rider stood on the other side.

"How did you know I was back in town already?"

Rider chuckled as he walked inside, closing the door. "Because you told Junelle after you landed, who told me. I was on my way home and thought I'd get the details of how it went in person." Rider eyed the bag in his hand. "Did you just get home?"

"Yeah, dude. You didn't even let me get to my bedroom to put my bag down."

And clearly that wouldn't be happening for a while yet, so he tossed his bag to the floor and headed toward the kitchen.

"Beer?"

"Yep." Rider took a seat at the island counter, nodding in thanks at the cold drink placed in front of him. "So? Tell me everything."

"Where do I start?"

Rider took a sip, grinning from ear to ear. "Anywhere, dude. You never up and leave for a full week. Nor does Jo. So start anywhere. I need to know what happened."

While Jason wanted to do that, some parts of it wasn't his story to tell.

"If I tell you some things, it stays between us."

The look Rider gave him said he'd have a hard time keeping it from Junelle. Before Victoria, Jason wouldn't have understood that. But now he did. Sharing that level of honesty and trust and keeping nothing from your partner brought a relationship to an even deeper level.

Plus, it was his sister they were talking about. No doubt he'd tell Junelle himself at some point because he didn't keep secrets from his sister either.

"Okay, promise me it stays between us and Junelle."

Rider laughed. "Always, man. Always."

So he started from the beginning. Victoria breaking down in his apartment and thinking he would let her leave without him. To the very end where they left Jake in Neptune with his brother, not feeling better, but looking more human. He'd even met Mindy, who had been in the city the entire time with them, but hanging out with her friends. She had wanted to give Jake space. Not crowd him too much. As soon as he arrived in Neptune, she'd been in his face so much, Jason thought Jake wanted to move back to the city.

He even confessed they'd taken their relationship up a notch. Though he didn't go into all the details. Some things were better left unsaid. His sex life was one of them.

"That's a lot to unpack there. Like, holy shit. I mean, I knew her brother died because she took two weeks off work a few months ago, but I didn't know all the dirty details about it."

Jason drained half his beer. "Right. It's a lot to take in. Once you get to know Jake, he's not so bad. I can't even imagine how he's feeling. That he had to kill his best friend." Jason stared at Rider for a long beat, then tore his gaze away. "I can't imagine shooting you, man."

"Plus, do you even know how to shoot a gun?"

They both chuckled, which Jason figured was the point. Rider trying to make light of a horrifying situation.

"The one thing I enjoyed hearing was you and Jo getting closer. That woman works so much, I thought it might mess with your relationship."

Well, Jason would admit, it wasn't always easy. He tried to be understanding and cool about the times she had to ditch and leave. Would he always be like that? He'd like to think so. But there could be times where he'd let his irritation show. No one could be accommodating twenty-four-seven.

"Before you knocked, my mind was talking crazy to me." Jason chuckled, then took another sip of beer.

"What kind of crazy?" Worry coated Rider's eyes. "Hey, I'm not going to pretend we have an easy job to deal with, but Jo's worth it. She makes you happy. Don't give up on her yet. Because you have a look on your face like you might be. Which is odd after the story you told me."

He fiddled with the label on the bottle, shaking his head. "Not that kind of crazy. More like I was thinking about looking at rings."

Rider's eyes widened in surprise.

"Yeah, crazy, I know. We've been dating for three months. Talk me off the ledge, man. One week together in a small, shared space does not mean I should be thinking about an engagement ring. Right?"

"Dude, if you're thinking about that kind of future with her already, then you're not crazy. Go buy a ring."

A strangled laugh left his lips. "I did not expect you to say that. I haven't known her that long."

"Yeah, but love makes us do ludicrous things sometimes. You can't help how you feel. If it's already feeling like she's the one you can see spending the rest of your life with, then she is. End of story. The moment I fell in love with your sister, I knew she was it for me. Even those five years apart, I knew I'd never love another woman. Not when I still loved Junelle. And hey." Rider smirked over the rim of his beer. "I have known Jo a lot longer than you have. She's a keeper. I've always liked and respected her. You couldn't do any better."

"But is it too soon for her?"

Rider winced. "Now *that* is a good question. Only you can answer that. Because you're starting to know her better than I do."

Yeah, and that was his big worry. He might be ready for a big leap, but Victoria was nowhere near it.

She'd jumped one hurdle, dealing with Jake. He needed to give her time to settle back into their everyday life and then he'd spring it on her.

No. He'd ease her into the idea. Pop in comments here and there.

Then he'd surprise her with a romantic dinner.

Like he attempted to do before they flew to Minnesota.

Yep.

That's what he'd do.

SHE WAS READY FOR A HOT, relaxing bath. Traveling sucked. Airports were horrible. Being away from your own bed was not pleasant. All Jo wanted to do was unwind and relax. Considering she hadn't had a bath in over a week, she was due for one.

But she couldn't complain how the trip went. She'd accomplished a lot. Jake still wasn't back to his old self, and he never would be. Even she had changed after her brother died. It was impossible to go back to the old way of life. But he was on a better path, and that's all she could ask for.

They'd gotten up early in the morning to head to the airport, which had been a very long drive. Another two hours waiting for their flight to take off. Once in the air, another two hours and forty minutes, give or take. Considering they flew in close to rush-hour, traffic had been horrible.

But peace and quiet was near her fingertips.

She hadn't received a text from Jason yet that he'd gotten home. Not that he said he'd text. She figured he would though.

They'd taken a new path in their relationship this past week. She felt so much closer to him than she had to anyone else in her life. That included her brother—and Jake.

Because not once, over the course of their trip, had she

felt like she couldn't be honest with Jason. She'd poured her heart out multiple times, especially when they got back to their hotel room and could speak freely. She had even cried a few times, and he had held her each time, letting her get it all out. The support he'd shown her would never be forgotten. It had made her fall that much more in love with him.

Boy, Ivy would be surprised by the turn of events. She'd told a man she loved him.

She stepped off the elevator, the sounds of her suitcase wheels the only noise in the apartment hallway. Besides the jingling of her keys as she dug them out of her purse.

Past five o'clock already, Ivy would be at home. But not for long because she loved the nightlife. It was rare that she stayed home any night.

She tried the doorknob, finding it unlocked. Ivy was home.

Her keys jingled again as she threw them back in her purse, then she opened the door.

"I'm back! I have so much to tell you."

Because who was she kidding? She wouldn't be able to keep anything to herself. At least, not the progress she made with Jason. The issues with Jake, she didn't want to talk about. Jo knew Ivy didn't like Jake and never had any nice things to say about him. They would never agree, so she'd avoid that topic at all costs.

She shut the door, set her suitcase to the side, and tossed her purse on the table.

Silence filled the room.

"Ivy?"

Jo pulled her phone out of her purse so she could text Jason. But she didn't open the message app.

"Ivy, you home?"

She better be home because the door had been

unlocked. Though Ivy wasn't generally careless like that, leaving the apartment unprotected, she had done it a few times.

They had a small apartment. The kitchen, dining room, and living room were all one big space. Ivy wasn't in the area. Her purse was on the island counter, her phone sitting next to it.

The shower.

Of course, that's why she wasn't answering.

Jo ventured down the short hallway, slowing down as she neared the bathroom. The door was open and the lights were off.

Not in the bathroom.

"Ivy?"

Ivy's bedroom door was closed. Jo knocked softly, on the off-chance she was sleeping. Of course that would be an odd occurrence for her. But why else hadn't she responded yet?

"Ivy?" she spoke through the door. "Are you okay?"

No one answered. No tiny sounds could even be heard behind the door.

She hated to bother her if she wanted to be alone, but Jo's gut gurgled with unease. Something wasn't right. This wasn't normal behavior for her roommate.

Her hand gripped the doorknob, shaking as she twisted it. She hated the nerves that bounced to the surface.

The door swung open.

She stumbled back, covering her hand over her mouth.

Ivy lay sprawled on her bed, naked, vacant eyes staring at the ceiling. Even with the lights out in the room, she could see the bruises around her neck. She'd been strangled.

"Oh, God, Ivy!" She backed up until she hit the wall behind her. It was the only thing that kept her on her feet.

Jo knew she should move closer, make sure she was dead, but she couldn't find the will to move. To see her friend's brutality up close and personal.

But she had to.

If nothing else, this was her job. This was what she did every day. Well, to be fair, she didn't work homicides. But she worked violent crimes, and this fit that category.

With trembling legs, she moved forward.

It took far longer than it should've to reach her side.

There was no point checking for a pulse. No life shined back at her as she stared into Ivy's eyes.

Clothes were scattered around the room, though that was typical of Ivy. She wasn't the neatest roommate on the planet. She switched on her phone's flashlight function to check everything else out. She didn't want to touch anything, to contaminate any evidence, and even a small touch on the light switch could be a problem.

Everything looked normal.

No signs of a struggle, as if whoever had killed her had gotten the upper hand very quickly.

Her hand paused when the light hit Ivy's dresser mirror. Jo moved closer to read the message scrawled in lipstick.

Your boyfriend didn't interrupt me this time.

Holy. Shit.

Jo scrambled out the room so fast, she stumbled into the hallway. Somehow, she made her way out of the apartment and into the hallway.

With shaky fingers, she found Rider's number.

"Hey, Jo, what's up?"

She inhaled a harsh breath, and instead of words, a cry tore out of her.

"Jo?" Rider's affable demeanor vanished. "What's wrong? Talk to me?"

"I need you, Rider," she whispered. "Please come to my apartment."

Then the phone slipped from her fingers. She buried her face in her hands, the sobs tearing out of her as if a demon was being torn from her body.

13

THE PHONE DIDN'T NEED to be on speaker for Jason to hear Victoria crying.

"Jo? Jo, answer me!" Rider stood up from his stool. "Jo, can you hear me?" Then Rider looked at him. "I don't know what's wrong."

Jason rounded the counter. "Well, clearly something is. Let's go."

They made it out of his apartment in a flash. At some point, the call dropped because Rider put his phone back in his pocket.

"Why did she call you and not me?" Jason hated to voice it, but the question burned in his gut too much not to ask.

Rider shrugged. "Dude, I have no idea. She didn't sound right. Something happened."

No shit! Though Jason didn't say it out loud. He couldn't understand why she'd call Rider if something happened and not him. After this past week, she should know she could rely on him. It made no sense.

Here he was contemplating buying a ring and he wasn't

even the first person she called when something went wrong.

They made it to her apartment as fast as they could, which to his irritation took far longer than he liked. Traffic sucked!

They found her in the hallway on the floor, her apartment door wide open.

"Victoria," he said quietly as he knelt by her. "What happened, sweetheart?"

She turned her head in slow motion until her red-rimmed eyes hit his. Even though she looked directly at him, he knew she wasn't processing who was in front of her.

"Hey, it's okay. Whatever it is, it's okay." He brushed a tender hand across her cheek. "We're here. Rider and me. We're both here."

She blinked rapidly, then frowned. "Jason?" A heavy breath released as she finally realized who knelt by her. Rider stood behind him, waiting for more information. "Oh, Jason!"

Then she threw herself into his arms, the tears resuming.

He said nothing as he held her, rubbing her back, trying to soothe her as best as he could. A neighbor exited their apartment, staring at the commotion. Rider smiled, waving them to continue on their way.

The last thing Jo needed was people seeing her break down like this.

"Victoria, why don't we go inside—"

"No!" She sat up, shaking her head. "No one can go in there. It's..." Her lips trembled as silent tears trailed down her cheeks. "It's a crime scene."

Jason looked up at Rider, whose expression had gone from cordial to work-mode in a heartbeat.

Well, one question was answered. She called Rider over him because he was a detective.

Victoria cleared her throat, wiping at her cheeks. Then using his shoulders as leverage, she stood up. Jason took his time getting to his feet, unsure of where to go from here. She'd found her strength again. As each second passed, the woman who'd called in tears was disappearing and the woman who'd arrested him without an ounce of compassion was emerging.

"I got home, the door was unlocked. Ivy wasn't in the main area. I found her in her bedroom. She's been strangled." She swallowed and licked her lips. "I touched the doorknob to open her door, but I didn't turn on the lights. I'm sure it will be revealed she was raped. It's the same man from three months ago. The one who killed the woman at your construction site. He left a note for me." She steeled her shoulders, wiping her cheeks once more. "Your boyfriend didn't interrupt me this time."

Jason flinched.

"Shit," Rider mumbled under his breath.

The bastard had been watching them. How else could he know that he was dating Victoria? Goose bumps rushed across his skin. And not because her roommate was dead. Because they'd been watched and had no clue at any point.

"I didn't pay close attention in the beginning, but based off my first glance of things, everything looked fine. As if Ivy let him in. I didn't see signs of a struggle anywhere." She cleared her throat. "Though we didn't find any evidence of a struggle at Rowena's place either."

"I'll handle this, Jo," Rider said. "I'll call Tate and Stromberg. They'll help. This bastard won't get away with this."

"And yet, he already has. Ivy paid the price for my incompetence."

"Jo…" Rider whispered as she turned around and walked toward the stairwell exit. "You should follow her. I'll call for reinforcements." Then he lowered his voice. "And clearly this asshole has been watching you two. She shouldn't be alone."

Well, duh! He wasn't about to let her go off on her own. Especially after some psycho broke in and killed her roommate.

He followed her without a word as they made their way to the lobby. Victoria greeted the doorman, Stu.

"When's the last time you saw Ivy?"

Stu rubbed his chin. "Last night, I think. I haven't seen her yet today."

"And did she arrive with anyone?"

"Na. She came home from work, alone, as usual. I don't recall her leaving though, and you know Ivy, she goes out every night."

Victoria nodded that she agreed.

"Something wrong?"

She flashed a pretty smile, but Jason could tell it was her detective smile, fake and artful where she'd guide the conversation where she wanted it to go.

"Did Ivy chat about anything with you?"

Stu shook his head. "Typical greeting. What's going on, Jo?"

"Anyone enter the building last night who was not a resident?"

"A few people visiting other residents."

"Any of those people visit Ivy?"

"No, none for her." Stu frowned. "I'm not sure why you're asking all these questions."

"I'm going to need a list of every visitor that logged in last night."

"Well—"

"And while you're at it, Stu, I will need the surveillance video for the lobby and our hallway floor for last night from the moment Ivy arrived home until now."

"This feels serious, Jo," Stu stated. "I think I need to call my manager first."

The guy had no idea how serious the matter was. But that was because Victoria wasn't giving him the real reason why.

"Okay, I will wait."

Stu left the area.

"Victoria—"

"Jason." She touched his shoulder with that same flashy detective smile. He didn't like it when she used that expression on him. "Why don't you go home? I'm fine now. There's a lot that needs to be done."

Was she serious?

She wanted him to leave.

Five minutes ago, she'd been crying in his arms. Now she was acting like she hadn't been doing that.

"Are you even allowed to work this case? Feels like a conflict of interest."

The nasty glare she delivered said he'd stepped over a line he shouldn't have. But what the hell? Didn't she see how she should come home with him? Dealing with her roommate's death was the last thing she should be doing.

"I'll worry about that. But you don't have a reason to be here. So go home."

"How about I'm here because my girlfriend's roommate was brutally murdered. I'm here because she needs me. I'm here because she shouldn't be alone. I'm here because I care about her!"

Victoria flinched at his outburst, yet the stoic expression on her face remained. "You're speaking in third person. Did you know the word bookworm was derived from actual insects and larvae eating away at the bindings and pages of a book? It originated in the sixteenth century, and over time, people were referred to as a bookworm when they 'devoured' book after book after book like the insects did."

Okay. He was coming on strong. She was reverting to quoting facts, which meant her nerves were poking through. He had to tread carefully here.

"I'm sorry. I didn't mean what I said. I think—"

"Jason, I don't have time to hear what you think. Please go home."

Then she turned her back on him and walked through the same doorway that Stu had disappeared through.

He wasn't wanted here. He should've known that from the beginning. She'd called Rider over him.

So much for ruminating about buying a ring.

"Jo, what are you still doing here?"

She looked up from the chair where she sat in the lobby to see Stromberg.

"I'm..." She had no idea why she was still hanging around. She should've left when Jason had, though he didn't leave until more police personnel arrived and she glared so hard it was easy for him to vacate the premises.

Reinforcements had arrived quickly, or at least, it felt fast. One minute she was looking at surveillance video with

Tate, and the next she was taking a seat and...and staring into space.

Stromberg took a seat in the open chair next to her. "This is a lot to take in. You don't need to be here."

Translated into she shouldn't be here. But where would she go? She couldn't spend the night in her apartment. She had no idea if she could ever walk back inside.

And she couldn't go to Jason's. Not after the way she treated him.

Why had she spoken to him so harshly? She couldn't even explain it to herself.

"I don't know—" She broke off finishing her sentence when the door opened and two officers walked inside. Officer Benson and Dorenson. They waved, offering a lame smile her way, and continued toward the elevator.

So many police personnel had come and gone. Too many, it felt like. She'd never noticed before how many cops showed up at a crime scene. Were they all even needed? Or did some like to come for the thrill? Officer Benson and Dorenson, for example. They weren't needed here. There was no reason for them to show up.

What was thrilling about seeing a dead body? About seeing death and destruction right in your face?

"There's a lot of hours to go through with the surveillance video. We'll get this guy. I promise you."

She sent Stromberg a wry grin. "You shouldn't promise such things to the victim's friends or family. What happens if you can't keep that promise?"

He winced at his obvious mistake. "I can't stand to see you like this, Jo. If I have to turn this city upside down, I will to keep that promise."

"Thanks, Stromberg. I appreciate all of you coming."

He scoffed as if he couldn't believe she said such a thing. "Get away from here, Jo. Go to Jason's. You've done enough tonight. I'll find someone to drive you."

If only she could go to Jason's.

Stromberg left her alone and her thoughts went dark in an instant. Picturing Ivy's naked, bruised body. The way she'd been sprawled on the bed like a piece of her clothing tossed haphazardly in the room. The lifelessness that stared back at her. Ivy had been so full of life. So exuberant. It was hard to picture it not there.

She could feel the panic rising. The same feeling she felt as she stumbled out of her apartment. The same emotion that attacked her when the sobs tore out of her chest.

Her fingers fumbled with her phone screen before finding the number she shouldn't call.

"Hey, Jo. You make it home?" Jake's soothing voice settled some of the panic threatening to overwhelm her.

A tiny cry escaped.

"What's wrong?" His voice went on alert.

"Everything. It's all wrong." Then she proceeded to share everything that happened since she walked through her door.

"Ah, shit, Jo. I'm so sorry to hear that. Ivy..." He sighed. "I can be on the next flight."

"No, no, don't do that. There isn't much you could do."

"Except be there for my friend. I can do that. Like she did for me."

There someone went, speaking in third person again.

Instead of jumping down his throat like she'd done with Jason, she let out another whimper. But the tears didn't escape.

"You don't have to."

"No shit. I want to."

Laughter emerged.

"There we go. That's what I want to hear."

"I messed up with Jason."

Jake chortled. "Yeah, right. That man loves you. He knows you're hurting and you didn't mean anything you said or did. You get a pass."

"One-time pass? Because this isn't the first time I've screwed up with him. How many passes am I allowed?"

Because she doubted this would be the last time she pushed him away. Not because she had wanted to. But this job...it took a toll on a person. She didn't always handle things the proper way. She couldn't claim she'd never do it again, as much as she hated to admit it.

"You get as many as you want because he knows you are worth it. That you're a keeper and he'd be dumb to not realize that."

A heavy breath left her mouth. "You're saying that because you're my best friend and you have to."

Her only best friend now.

Because her other one was murdered.

Brutally, sadistically murdered.

"Stay with me, Jo. I know where your thoughts are taking you and you need to stop it right now. Don't do this to yourself. Don't do what I did. I let myself fall into that dark pit of despair and I nearly didn't make it out. Do you hear me? I let it consume me. Don't let it take control of you."

"And if he slams the door on my face?"

Because he'd have every right to if she showed up at his apartment.

"Then he's the stupidest man on the planet and he never deserved you."

"Thanks, Jake."

For so many things, but that would suffice for the time being.

"Hang in there, Jo. You got this."

She hung up, not believing she had a grapple on anything.

"Detective Johansen, do you have a moment?"

Jo looked up to see Chuck Moren from *The New York Chronicle*. She was never surprised when the news showed up to a crime scene. But it was the first time she despised it with every breath in her.

"You know I can't speak about an active investigation, Chuck." She stood up, forcing a professional congenial twist of her lips out. "You also know you can't go any further than this lobby."

He threw out what she figured he thought was a charming smile and waved a hand toward Stu, who sat behind his desk. "He already told me I couldn't go any further. Out of everyone, you know I tend to follow the rules."

Yeah, sure, she'd give him that. He wasn't as pushy as some of the other crime reporters that popped up at one of her crime scenes or at the precinct.

"One question. I swear."

"And it doesn't matter what it is, I have no comment."

He laughed. "Gonna ask anyway. You work violent crimes, not homicide. So why are you here? Did someone survive the attack? It's not clear what happened."

She knew most of the crime reporters had their own radios, listening to the police scanners. She'd have to thank every officer and detective who spoke over the radio that they didn't give away she lived here or that the victim had been her roommate. They'd been very tight-lipped over the radio.

She'd buy everyone cupcakes and cookies in thanks.

"No comment, Chuck."

Then she walked around him and out of the building. To the last place she was wanted.

Jason's.

14

A SOFT KNOCK on his door had him looking up from his phone. Jason had been fiddling with the device since he'd returned home. Typing and deleting sentence after sentence.

Victoria had been very clear about how she felt. He hadn't been wanted so he shouldn't even be trying to formulate a text to her.

The unexpected distraction was welcome.

He set down his phone on the coffee table in front of him, circled it, and made his way to the door.

Victoria stood on the other side, apprehension written all over her features.

"I know you don't want me here, and I—"

Jason took ahold of her hand, pulling her inside his apartment, swinging the door shut behind them. "The last thing I want to hear is any kind of apology or what you think I want or don't want."

He loosened his hold on her hand, realizing he'd been gripping it hard. Then he brought his other hand to her cheek, caressing it. "You lost your roommate tonight. In the worst possible way. I'd be worried if you didn't react in any way. So whatever is on your mind, get it out. Holler, scream, cry, I don't care. Nothing you do or say is going to make me angry."

Her bottom lip trembled, yet no tears escaped. Then she moved closer until her head hit his chest. He wrapped his arms around her, holding her tight.

"I don't deserve your kindness right now. I'm sorry for how I acted."

He shifted away, cupping her cheeks. "I told you not to apologize." Grabbing her hand again, he guided her to the couch and wrapped her in his arms. "I'm glad you came. I've been going back and forth bugging you with a text, not even sure what the hell to say."

A sharp ring joined the conversation.

Victoria dug her phone out of her purse, wincing. "Hey, Stromberg." Silence from her, but nodding her head as he said something. "I wasn't thinking. I didn't mean to leave without saying goodbye. I'm at Jason's right now. I'm fine." More silence on her end. "Yes, of course. I'll talk to you tomorrow."

She hung up and tossed her phone to the side.

"He's mad at me too."

"Hey." Jason brushed his hand over her cheek, guiding her to look at him. "I'm not mad at you. I'm sure he isn't either."

"Then why did he ream me out for leaving by myself?"

Jason's heart skipped a beat at the thought. "Because a damn psycho murdered your roommate, and he's been watching us. How else did he know we were dating? Do I like knowing you came here by yourself? No. I hate thinking about it. So I get why he sounded upset. It's because he's worried about you. Like I am. Like all of us are."

A shiver wracked her body. "It is disconcerting he must've been watching us. What level of madness do you have to be at to do something so vicious?"

"Sometimes there's no understanding someone and their actions. Don't do that to yourself trying to figure it out."

Her head found a spot on his shoulder. "I'm not sure I'm going to be able to ever step foot in that place again. I don't know how I'm ever going to close my eyes and not see Ivy laying there like that."

"Tell me what you need and I'll get it. You're welcome to stay here for as long as you need."

Forever was fine with him. Because hell, he'd been thinking about rings. Why would moving in be too soon?

"Thank you, Jason." Her arms enveloped him, squeezing hard. "I'm glad you don't hate me."

He kissed the top of her head. "I would never hate you." Especially over something like this.

They sat there for the longest time in silence, holding each other. Despite her thinking she wouldn't fall asleep, she did. He didn't want to move her and wake her up, but he also didn't want her to get a sore neck or back or anything, so he gently lifted her up and carried her to his room.

The exhaustion of the day had hit her hard because she made a few moaning sounds but didn't wake up. The most he did was remove her shoes. Then he slid under the covers after tossing his clothes off and snuggled with her.

The morning arrived far sooner than he wanted, and Victoria was still out like a light. He made sure the curtains were shut before closing the door without a sound to leave her to sleep.

A quick call to his foreman to tell him he wouldn't be in—still—and then he started brewing coffee and making a bite to eat.

A knock on his door startled him as he was pouring his first cup.

Rider again, no doubt.

Another shock hit his system when he opened the door to Jake. He looked as tired as he felt, despite getting more sleep than he thought he would.

"Come on in. Coffee?"

Jake nodded and tossed a bag near the door, following him into the kitchen.

"Victoria's still sleeping." Jason pushed a full cup to his side of the counter. "Surprising actually. She's been out since she fell asleep last night. She was afraid she wouldn't get any."

"Don't worry. Those nights will come," Jake replied with little inflection before taking a small sip. "She called me last night. Told me everything."

It was the way he said *everything* that made Jason think she'd even informed Jake of the way she'd treated him.

"I figured as such." Obviously. How else would Jake have known to come? Because any other reason sounded ridiculous, especially since they'd recently gotten him settled in his new home. "How'd you know you'd find her here?"

She could've rented a hotel room or something. Since Jason knew she hadn't looked at her phone all night, he knew Jake had no contact with her from the moment she arrived at his place.

"Lucky guess. I knew she'd come to her senses and come here." Jake gripped the mug, staring at the hot liquid. "You know anything she might say or do is the grief talking, right? She doesn't mean it." He lifted his gaze. "It doesn't make it okay, but I'm asking you to give her a grace period. She loves you. She doesn't mean to lash out."

Jason knew that, but he understood why Jake felt the need to put it out there. Because he'd acted the same way. Victoria had given him the grace he didn't deserve.

"I know that."

Jake nodded, satisfied.

Then Jason's brows crinkled in confusion. "How do you know where I live?"

A wily smirk punctured his lips. "I do have good detective skills when I choose to use them."

Okay. Cryptic, but whatever. It wasn't something Jason wanted to argue about.

"I don't have a spare room." He tossed his head toward the couch. "But the couch isn't so bad. You're free to use it."

It was that or pay the astronomical prices at a hotel room somewhere in the city.

"Appreciate it."

Jason leaned his forearms on the counter. "How long do you plan on staying?"

Jake shrugged. "I'm in-between jobs, so it doesn't matter. I mean, I do have an interview with the Neptune Police Department in two days, but Jo comes first. I never want her to think that she doesn't matter to me. Not after the way I ignored her the way I did. I have a lot of making up to do with her." Then Jake narrowed his eyes. "Is there an expiration date for the use of your couch?"

Laughter filled the air. "Before I met you, with what Victoria told me, I wouldn't have even let you inside my apartment."

"I didn't bring my gun if that's what you're worried about." The shit-eating grin on Jake's face said he was joking. Jason didn't appreciate the sense of humor. Having a gun in his face was not something he wanted to repeat.

"*But*," Jason emphasized since Jake didn't let him finish, "you're not so bad. Even with the whole pointing a gun at me thing. You're welcome to stay as long as you want." Jason straightened. "For as long as Victoria needs you. Because that's the bottom line here. What Victoria needs."

Jake's eyes glittered with an emotion Jason had a hard time deciphering. Until he spoke. "I knew the moment you took that weapon from my hands that I liked you. That you have guts. I will always respect that."

This was the moment he and Jake became friends. Once a friend of his, there was nothing he wouldn't do for the person.

SHE ROLLED OVER, putting her hand out, meeting nothing but coldness. Blinking a few times first, she then opened her eyes.

Alone.

In the dark.

Where was Jason? What time was it?

She bolted upright, her heart pounding in her chest. Then a sigh of relief hit her when she saw a pocket of sunlight pouring through above the curtains. Not evening. Not actual darkness surrounding her. She didn't even know why the panic had hit her.

She was still dressed in yesterday's clothes, and since she didn't bring anything with her, she had nothing to change into. Her gaze glided to his closet. Or maybe she did.

Undressing quickly, she snatched some of Jason's clothes before she could change her mind. They'd turned a corner in their relationship. They exchanged vows of love. He would not care she was pilfering his closet.

At least, she hoped he wouldn't.

She said a silent prayer he also had a spare toothbrush because she didn't even have those kind of essentials with her either. Making a store run later would be imperative.

When she entered the main area, Jason stood at the counter, mixing something in a pan.

"Morning." The gentle smile on his face made the panic she'd experienced in his room lessen even more.

"Good morning." Then her attention shifted to Jake, who sat at the counter. "What a surprise to see you."

"A good surprise, I hope," Jake replied as he stood up and grabbed a hug from her. "I'm here for you. For whatever you need from me."

She appreciated his support, but he hadn't needed to come all the way here. Her head bobbed that she understood, then he let go and took a seat again. She grabbed the one next to his.

Jason snatched another plate from the cupboard and set it in front of her. His eyes glazed with desire. "You look good in my shirt." Then he swiveled back toward the stove, stirring the contents again.

Her face flamed with heat, and she forced herself not to look at Jake. Though she heard his chuckle all the same.

She'd also put on a pair of his sweats, tying the drawstring as tight as it could go. They were comfy. She might keep them for herself.

Idle chit-chat commenced while Jason finished cooking breakfast. Then delicious food was put before her. Eggs, bacon, orange juice, toast, and hash browns. Her mouth salivated at the picture. Then her taste buds moaned in ecstasy.

Jake delivered a snort, and she realized she moaned out loud.

"Thank you, Jason. This is amazing."

He grinned, shoveling bites of food into his mouth.

"I hope you have a spare toothbrush for me."

"I do. I even have a shaver if you need it. Junelle keeps a bunch of stuff here, just in case, for herself."

"Perfect. I'm going to shower after this and then head to the precinct."

Jason's fork clinked as it hit his plate. The stormy expression on his face wasn't hard to decipher that he didn't like her decision.

"What are you going to do there?"

"There's a killer that needs to be caught. I also have a high caseload. Other cases that need my attention."

A muscle bunched in his cheek as he clenched his jaw. "It wouldn't hurt to take a day off."

"I had a whole week off. I don't need another day."

"Your roommate—" Jason stopped, then swallowed hard. "You know what's best for you." Then he twisted around, dropping his plate in the sink, half his food consumed. "I'll take a quick shower first."

Then he left the room.

"He can't expect me not to do anything."

Jake didn't respond at first, and Jo wanted to shake him by the shoulders, demanding he say something. Then a heavy sigh echoed between them.

"I don't think it's that, Jo. He's worried about you, and you're acting like nothing happened."

She twisted her head his way. "No, I'm not."

"You sounded a little too chipper to be going into work. No one expects you to show up today. And you know you can't work the case. She was your roommate."

But she wanted to. She *needed* to.

"I can't sit around, Jake. I can't be idle. My mind will play tricks on me and..." She pushed her plate away, losing her appetite. "I need to keep busy."

"I get that. I do. I should've done the same thing after..." His expression turned dark, thoughts of Wally, no doubt, puncturing his mind. "But I didn't keep busy. I let the pain consume me." His lips curled upward, but she saw the sadness in his eyes. "So you don't have to explain yourself to me, but Jason's not going to understand. He doesn't know this way of life. He wants to feel needed, and you're not giving him what he wants. You're leaving him, showing him you're strong and capable to handle the situation thrown at you."

"So you're telling me I need to cater to his feelings more than mine?"

Jake chuckled, shaking his head. "No, absolutely not. Us men are fickle creatures. We can't help it. I would never tell you to compromise who you are for a man. Never. He needs an extra amount of reassurance that you're okay. He'll never admit it out loud—at least, I wouldn't—but he's terrified. He doesn't want to lose you."

And she didn't want to lose him. Since last night, after the huge blow she'd taken, she'd done nothing but do or say the wrong thing with him.

"Okay." She stood up. "I'll go give him some extra reassurance."

A sly smirk built on Jake's face. "I'll cover my ears."

She slapped his shoulder. "Not that kind of reassurance." Though as she walked to the bathroom, it wasn't a bad thought.

A light tap on the bathroom door didn't elicit a response, so she took matters in her own hands and opened the door.

The shower curtain was closed, the water running. When it didn't move aside, she knew Jason hadn't heard her come in. Her clothes fell to the floor, then she swung the curtain to the side to step into the shower.

Jason turned around at the sound, his eyes blazing with pleasure as they trailed up and down her body. Then his warm hands wrapped around her waist, pulling her closer until they were chest to chest and she could feel the water.

"You know I'll be okay at work. Nothing will happen to me."

His fingers tightened, his nails digging into her skin. "That's not true. Any day you leave for work, anything could happen. Life is unpredictable, and so is your job. I understand. I plan to live with that. But I won't let you say that to me when it's not true."

Fair enough. He made a good point.

"I need to keep busy. I don't want you mad at me because I'm going to work."

His brows furrowed. "I'm not mad, and I'm sorry if I gave you that impression. I'm worried about you. I want to help you in any way I can, and I feel like I'm not doing a good enough job."

Uh. Jake had been right.

"You're perfect, Jason. Everything you're doing is the right thing. I'll be home after work."

His eyes flared with possession and longing when she uttered the word home. He even clutched her a little tighter.

"Take Jake with you. Please."

She smiled. "To distract him, or to keep me safe?"

"A bit of both. It will be good for both of you." His lips caressed hers in a tender kiss as his hands smoothed across her ass, pulling her into his hard cock. "I won't worry as much."

An extra amount of reassurance. She could give him that. "I'll bring him with me."

"Good." Then Jason lifted her up and backed her against the wall. "You tend to get loud, sweetheart, but this is an opportunity I can't pass up. Will you keep it quiet if I slip inside?"

Considering Jake already assumed this would happen, she didn't think it mattered, but she nodded anyway.

They'd used condoms in the beginning of their trip, until she'd told him she was on the pill. He'd tossed the rest of the box away and they'd gone bare since.

The moment he entered her, crushing her body to the wall, she moaned in delight. Loudly.

"Shhh," he whispered against her lips, then turning it into a fiery kiss as he pumped in and out.

She clung to him, savoring the moment. Because every minute with him was a moment to treasure. He was right. Life was unpredictable, so nothing should be wasted.

His thrusts were deep and hard, his hands gripping her hips. Every time he pounded into her, the feeling of bliss ventured higher. She could feel the onset of an orgasm nearing too soon. It was a combination of so many things.

The way he held her. The way his hips moved. The hard, thorough thrusts. The possessive twist of his lips. It all spoke to her and her senses.

"So close, Jason," she mumbled between the kiss.

"Yes, sweetheart, come for me."

He grinded his hips in just the right way that she had no choice but to listen to his command. He swallowed the scream she would've let loose, his lips attached securely to hers. A few more firm thrusts and he was growling in delight himself, his body tensing and releasing all the pleasure they'd created.

He slowly put her back on her feet, but didn't let go.

"I love you, Victoria."

She swiped some of his wet hair off his forehead as she placed her hand over his heart. "I love you too."

She hoped her love for him and the love he felt in return would be enough to hold them together. Because she knew the tension that had spread in the kitchen wouldn't be the first time it enveloped them.

15

THIS WAS EVEN BETTER than he imagined.

When he'd come across Ivy on the dating website, knowing she was the detective's roommate, it had been like it was meant to be.

The stupid bitch was so easy to finagle a date. Of course, based on his little observation he'd done, she didn't seem to care who she slept with. Why not him too?

They'd had plans to meet at a bar, not near her apartment. At least she had some qualms about her safety. He had been the one to change the plans.

He chuckled under his breath, imagining the way the cops were trying to figure out how he'd gotten inside the building. He certainly hadn't entered through the front door and signed in. Did they think he was an idiot?

Ivy stuck to a pretty normal schedule. He knew she'd be home when he arrived. Knocking wasn't necessary because the element of surprise was part of the fun.

And again, she was pretty stupid. The window where the fire escape was had been unlocked. That also made the detective dumb as well. He'd slipped through the window with ease and without a sound.

Ivy had been in the shower, prepping herself for their date. How sweet.

He listened to the sound of the water running, then the clanking sound as she swooshed the curtain to the side. She even sung a happy tune as she did whatever she was doing in the bathroom.

When she opened the bathroom door and walked out, she didn't even notice him standing there. She'd walked out naked too. Made his job easier.

No sound left her lips when he surprised her from behind.

Because he didn't allow it.

He'd gotten the upper hand so fast, she had no chance to fight back. The entire encounter was glorious. From start to finish.

After the light left her eyes, he'd paused, seeing himself in the mirror. The hunt was over, and while he'd still felt some of the high from it, it hadn't been quite enough.

It had been an impulse to leave the message on the mirror for Detective Johansen. But a good one.

A new angle for him. Messing with the police like that. He found he enjoyed the taunting. It brought the game he played to an even higher level than before.

And as he walked into the precinct, walking among the cops, that in itself was another level to the game. They were all so stupid.

"Hey, Jerry," he said with an amiable smile and chipper tone.

"Hey, man. May wants to throw a Fourth of July party. You in? Tina too, of course."

"Yeah, sure. Can't wait."

The holiday was in two days. He had much to celebrate. It didn't even matter nobody else would know what he was truly celebrating.

What part of the game did he want to play now? That was the question he needed to answer.

A QUICK KNOCK SOUNDED, followed by the swish of his door opening and then a click of it closing.

"What are you doing?"

Jason looked up from the floor at his sister. "Cleaning."

It had to be obvious what he was doing. What a ridiculous question.

Junelle laughed. "Yeah, I got that. Why are you on the floor?"

Another obvious answer to that absurd question. "Cleaning the baseboard."

Junelle plopped down on his couch, cocking a brow. "Yes, idiot. I can see that. Why are you cleaning the baseboard? Nobody cleans that stuff."

"I do."

Maybe too much, but he'd never admit that.

She eyed the board running across the wall near the floor. "How many times have you wiped it clean today? It damn near sparkles from here. I bet if I get closer I'll be able to see my reflection."

"Har. Har."

He might've gone over it twice now. Just to make sure all the dust and dirt had been cleared away. That confession would never leave his mouth though.

Jason stood up, wiping his hands on his jeans after tossing the wet rag into the soapy bucket. "I'm done. You arrived in time." He walked around the couch toward the kitchen with the bucket of water. "Why are you here?"

"To check on you. Duh! Your girlfriend's roommate was murdered. Rider told me that Jo showed up at work and..." Junelle shoved to her feet and strolled to the kitchen. "You're cleaning, which means you're stressed. Which I knew would happen. I'm here for moral support."

While he appreciated it, he'd rather be alone. To stew on his thoughts. The things floating through his mind weren't for anyone's ears. At least, not yet.

Since the moment Victoria left, he'd gone from happy delight—the sex had been amazing—to wallowing in the pits of despair.

He felt so lost and confused with her. One minute they were so in sync with each other, he saw a happy and bright future. The next minute they were down each other's throats, making him see the end was neigh.

"I'm good, June. You don't have to worry about me."

She rolled her eyes. "I'm gonna anyway. Rider said they don't have any leads yet."

Well, that was news to him. It wasn't as if Victoria had called or texted giving him updates about the case. Not that that surprised him.

"What do they have?" He rested his back against the counter, crossing his arms.

Junelle stared at him for a beat, obviously processing the fact Victoria wasn't sharing information.

"Surveillance shows nothing. Nobody walked inside her apartment or walked out of it besides Jo. Ivy was killed the day before she got home. Nobody, none of the residents on that floor, heard anything odd. No screams or anything. The coroner is putting her time of death around five to six o'clock that evening. A time when people would be arriving home. They collected a lot of prints, but I'm having doubts any will come back to the perp."

Jason laughed, hearing his sister talk like she was a cop herself. "You sure know a lot."

And he knew jack shit. The thought had him straightening up and turning around so his sister couldn't see the irritation on his face. He grabbed a cup from the cupboard as if that's why he turned in the first place.

"Want something to drink?"

"No."

He grabbed the pitcher of water from the fridge, pouring himself a glass. The liquid disappeared swiftly as he swallowed most of it in one large, long gulp. Then he refilled his glass.

"Jason, look at me."

His hand paused in midair, ready to down another glass.

Junelle waited in silence.

He set his glass on the counter with a loud thud and twisted around.

"Rider doesn't talk to me about his cases either."

"Well, he's sure chatty about this one with you."

"I badgered him about it."

Doubtful, but he didn't want to argue with his sister. Hell, he didn't want to argue with anyone, especially Victoria. And who knew, maybe when she got home tonight, she'd share all this information with him. Just because she hadn't reached out yet, didn't mean she planned to keep any of it from him.

And if she did, that was her right. He had no right to assume she would share anything work related with him, even though he burned deep inside to know it all.

"Is there a point you're trying to make, Junelle?"

"I can see you're upset—"

"I'm not upset." The grim set of his lips said otherwise, but he wasn't mad. Not at Victoria at any rate. His sister though, for pressing the issue? Yeah, he was getting kind of pissed off.

But his sister knew him well, and when to retreat. "I have the day off. It looks like you do too. And before you go clean the baseboard with another round of soapy water, let's go do something."

"Like what?"

Because he wasn't opposed to cleaning it for a third time. His bathroom could use another round of cleaning, and his kitchen counter didn't quite shine yet. When he could see his reflection in it, he'd be a bit more satisfied.

"I don't know. Bowling or something."

"Bowling?"

"Why not? It sounds like fun."

And all she wanted to do was get his mind off everything else.

"Yeah, okay. I'll kick your ass in bowling."

Junelle scoffed, getting up from her seat. "We'll see about that."

He changed his clothes, fixed his hair a bit, then left with his sister. The bowling alley wasn't packed, and he hadn't expected it to be at one o'clock in the afternoon.

They ordered food, drinks, and started playing. He wouldn't call himself an expert at bowling, but he wasn't a novice. Same went for Junelle, so it was a pretty even match.

"How was Minnesota?"

Interesting, to say the least.

"Good. We helped her friend move to the town where his brother is at. A change of scenery will be good for him."

"He's here now? At least, I think Rider said he was."

"Showed up this morning. It was nice to see. I know Victoria appreciates his support."

It surprised him Jake had made the trip. He was on his way from climbing out of the misery he'd fallen into.

"I'd love to meet him."

He wanted to question his sister on why, but refrained from doing so. It wasn't abnormal she wanted to meet him. Jake was a part of Victoria's life, who happened to be a part of his life.

"Sure. You and Rider can come over for dinner tonight."

"Good." She smiled, but the worry in her eyes was vibrant and clear.

In that moment, he couldn't keep it to himself.

"Why do you want to meet him?"

She moved closer, touching his shoulder in support. "The man killed Jo's brother. She doesn't hate him. Most people wouldn't be able to forgive that."

Jason couldn't agree more. But he understood the situation better. Jake had no choice in the matter. He hadn't wanted to kill Wally.

"She flew all the way to Minnesota to help him. Now he flew all the way here."

Unease coated his system, his brows drawing low. "What are you insinuating, Junelle?"

She sighed, sympathy all over her face. "Brother's best friend. Ring a bell to you?"

Like him and Rider, and his sister falling in love with his best friend. Was she seriously saying that Victoria secretly loved Jake as much as he loved her in return?

He'd never gotten that vibe from either one, but maybe Junelle was on to something. Victoria had called last night and Jake had come running.

"But she loves me. She told me that. Just this morning."

Junelle rubbed his arm, the sympathy not wavering. "And I'm sure she does."

The unspoken words his sister didn't voice was she loved Jake more.

"I'm sorry, Jason. I didn't mean to put more worry in your head. I want to meet him though. See the situation for myself." Her eyes changed from concern to rage in an instant. "Because no one hurts my brother. Not like that."

He smiled, pulling her into a hug. "Same, sis. Same."

Worry swam in his veins, but if it were true, there wasn't anything he could do about it. Love was a powerful thing. And if Victoria loved Jake more, he had no chance whatsoever to win her heart.

"What a douche," Jake mumbled as he tossed the case file he'd been looking at back onto her desk. "I'd like to go and arrest him."

Yeah, so would she. The guy had done a number on his pregnant girlfriend. But according to her, he hadn't touched one little finger on her. The neighbors reported screaming and loud noises coming through the walls. The bruises on her face and stomach said she'd been hit. In her words, she fell. Luckily for her, the baby was okay. The unlucky part would be when her boyfriend hit her again and the doctor report wouldn't come back as happy.

"Until she changes her story, or someone witnesses something, I can't do anything yet. But I'm not ready to close the case, which is why it's still on my desk." Jo grabbed the files Jake was trying to sort through and set them on the opposite side of the desk. "I'd appreciate it if you didn't mess with my filing system."

Jake grinned. "They were sitting in a pile on your desk. Not much of a system."

"That's what you think. Everything has its place and you're messing with it."

While she appreciated him coming to work with her and joining the real world, he was driving her up the wall! Like to the point she wanted to pull her hair out and not regret it.

The worst part wasn't even him messing up her files and asking too many questions about some of her cases. Not even close. The worst part was he, along with her damn co-workers, wouldn't let her near Ivy's case.

She wasn't naive. She understood why it was a conflict of interest for her to work on it. To even look at the contents filling the folder they'd created. But it didn't mean she liked it. Her best friend and roommate had been violated and murdered, and she wasn't allowed to do anything about it. It pissed her off. She knew for a fact none of them would stand to the side and let someone else handle it, so why did they think it was okay she had to stay away?

They'd barely even given her updates about the progress. All she knew was they hadn't arrested anyone for it yet.

"I'd like to help with something. Anything. Give me someone to call, at least."

She sighed, though made sure to add a smile. She wasn't annoyed by Jake's insistance to help. In fact, it lightened her heart around the worry she had for him. This was a good sign he was ready to get back to life.

Thumbing through her files, she paused on two. "Do you want an armed robbery or an aggravated assault?"

Jake rubbed his chin, a smirk filtering through. "Hit me with the armed robbery."

With that settled, they got to work. Maybe it was the worry about the psychotic killer having eyes on her, but she knew Jake was trying to keep her inside the precinct rather than on the streets. Which was fine with her. She had no desire to be out and about around people right now. A lot of the times, police work involved being behind a desk, making phone calls, chasing down witnesses and such via the phone. Researching things on the internet.

The day went faster than she thought it would and they were leaving for Jason's. She didn't see Tate, Stromberg, or Rider on her way out to ask how the case was progressing.

The aroma that hit her senses when they entered Jason's apartment made her mouth salivate. She didn't even care what he was cooking, but she knew whatever it was would be delicious.

"Hey, you two." Jason pointed with a spatula toward the fridge. "Grab a drink. It's not time to eat yet. Maybe another thirty minutes."

"I'm going to change."

Considering she was wearing yesterday's clothes she wore home on the plane, she felt disgusting. She had nothing to wear to work, and while she loved wearing Jason's clothes, it wasn't something she wanted to step out of his apartment wearing.

But now she could.

Her eyes watered the moment she walked into his room and saw her suitcase by the bed. At some point during the day, he'd gotten her belongings. At least the stuff she'd had with her while Ivy had been brutally attacked. Her suitcase filled with clothes she'd taken with her to Minnesota.

Instead of unzipping the case, she grabbed the clothes she'd slipped on this morning and took a shower. A bath would've been more her style after a day like today, but not with Jake here. Not with supper nearly ready.

The hot water soothed her somewhat, but not enough. When she put on Jason's shirt and sweatpants, some of the tension from the day dissipated.

A glass of wine was waiting for her on the kitchen counter. She took a seat next to Jake and watched Jason cook.

"We're getting salmon with a side of rice that looks so damn delicious and these rolls that he shoved in the toaster oven that I know I will eat more than one," Jake said, tipping his beer bottle in Jason's direction. "I like coming home to a home-cooked meal. Thank you very much."

"Not a problem." Jason flashed him a smile and went back to the stove where he was stirring the rice.

Jake sent her an awkward grin, and her senses went on alert. What had these two talked about while she'd been showering? There wasn't full-blown tension going on, but something was brewing in the air.

She took a sip of wine, pondering what could've been said.

"So, any news?" Jason twisted his head, his hand still stirring the contents. "Jake wouldn't tell me much."

Jake cleared his throat. "Not wouldn't. Couldn't. Because I don't know much."

Ah. That's where the tension was coming from.

"We only know that they haven't caught the guy yet," she added.

It pained her that even she didn't know much about the case.

Jason frowned and turned his attention back to the stove.

Jo sighed and, without thought, rested her head on Jake's shoulder.

"Well, Rider—" Jason stopped speaking when he turned back their way, his frown from moments before even deeper. His eyes narrowed as well. "Rider and Junelle are joining us for supper. They'll be here soon."

Then Jason put a lid over the pan on the stove and flashed a fake smile. "I have to use the bathroom. I'll be right back."

She lifted her head, staring after him. Then she looked at Jake, who was also staring after Jason, a frown marring his forehead. Before she could ask Jake about his thoughts concerning Jason's behavior, a knock sounded.

"I'll get it." She stood up.

Jake put a hand on her shoulder, shoving her back down. "Like hell. I will answer the door."

Then he stalked away before she could argue about it.

Did he think the killer would be brazen enough to knock on the door? At her boyfriend's house?

Well, duh. Because he'd shoved her pretty hard back to her seat. Could've even left a bruise on her shoulder he had squeezed so hard.

"Hello," Jo heard Junelle say, though couldn't quite see her as Jake stood in the way.

"Identification please."

"Umm..."

Jo laughed at Junelle's confusion and stood up. "Jake, that is Junelle, Jason's sister, and I'm sure Rider is standing right next to her. You met him today."

Jake stepped to the side with a wry grin and let them enter. "You can never be too careful."

She rolled her eyes. "Seriously. You met Rider earlier."

He cracked another smile, wider this time. "I didn't meet Junelle though."

Jo shook her head at his ridiculousness but couldn't stop the smile from breaking free. There was her friend. The one who could make her laugh without even trying. Getting on her nerves with ease. Making her feel like she was grounded to the earth when all she wanted to do was float away into her mind.

Junelle frowned, mirroring Jason's look from before, and then pulled her in for a hug. "I'm so sorry about Ivy. If there's anything I can do, I'm here for you."

Jo patted her awkwardly on the back, voicing her thanks, and then stepped away. She didn't think there was much Junelle could do for her. She barely knew the woman. Only things told to her by Rider. And of course, the one time she met her at the wedding.

"It's almost time to eat. Jason's in the bathroom. Did you know that most people use the bathroom about six to eight times a day, which means we're going to the bathroom about 2,500 times in one year. So if you take that number and total it—"

"Hey, Jo, why don't you grab Junelle and Rider a drink."

She stared at Jake for the longest time. Then her eyes drifted to his hand clutching her shoulder again. Grounding her back to earth.

"Right, a drink. We all need a drink. Did you know—"

"The kitchen is that way." Then Jake twisted her around by the shoulders and gave her a little push to get her on her way.

What would she do without her best friend? Probably keep spouting the most insane and ridiculous facts she could come up with.

While the random things that came out of her mouth never bothered Jake, he knew she'd hate herself for blurting out constant random things, especially in front of Jason's sister. She wanted the woman to like her. Not think her a complete idiot.

This was going to be the longest supper on the planet.

16

Jason wanted to snap at his sister, but of course, couldn't. Not without drawing attention to a situation that she should've never brought up.

Jake and Victoria having feelings for each other.

Since the moment Junelle put it in his head, he couldn't get it out.

It didn't help that Junelle kept throwing him looks, then gesturing with her eyes as if saying, "See what I told you."

And yes, he saw.

The little smiles Victoria and Jake shared with each other. The few times Jake would put a hand on her shoulder. The subtle way she'd look at him. The ease at which they laughed together.

Brother's best friend.

He had insider knowledge when it came to how that kind of thing turned out. *His* best friend married his sister!

The longer the night wore on, the more he came to realize he was in a losing battle with Victoria.

He couldn't compete with a best friend. Not one that had been in her life far longer than he had. The intimacy between the two couldn't be ignored. The familiarity. The connection they shared.

And he was the moron that brought them back together.

He could only blame himself.

Besides that aggravation coating the meal, it was pleasant. Not one word about Ivy punctured the conversation. Jason wasn't sure how he felt about that. On one hand, he was grateful they didn't talk about death and mayhem. On the other hand, he didn't like how he was being left out of the loop. Even his sister had known more about the case than he had.

It also concerned him how Victoria was handling her grief. Because she wasn't. If he'd met her for the first time, he would never have thought she'd just lost her roommate to a brutal crime.

When it was time for Rider and Junelle to leave, he walked them to the door and even stepped outside and closed it.

"You okay?" Rider asked, confusion written on his face that he'd left the apartment.

"Yeah. I'm fine."

Rider's brows drew low, still puzzled. Hell, he was confused himself. Why *had* he walked outside the door with them?

Junelle put a hand on his shoulder, as if her comfort would do anything to stop the turmoil going on inside his heart.

"I'm sorry."

He gave a half-hearted shrug. "It's fine."

Because what else could he do? There was no defeating the kind of relationship those two had.

Did Victoria and Jake love each other? Had it been obvious for everyone to see?

Yes, they did. Yes, it had.

"I'm missing something here. What is it?" Rider asked, crossing his arms. Gone was the confusion and replaced with a touch of annoyance. As if he couldn't believe he'd been left out of the loop of something.

"I'll explain on the way home."

But Rider shook his head, firming his stance as if anticipating Junelle trying to make him leave. "Nope. You can share it now."

Maybe it wasn't such a bad idea to ask Rider his thoughts. Get a third opinion. Because he didn't like his thoughts on it or what Junelle saw either.

"What do you think about Jake?"

Rider shrugged. "I haven't been around him long enough to make a decent assessment. He seems all right. A bit rough around the edges, but given what he's been through, I get it."

So not a bad guy was what Jason heard.

"And him and Victoria? Like...you know."

Rider's brows puckered so low, it scrunched up his whole face. "I don't know. What the hell are you trying to say?"

"He is her brother's. Best. Friend."

It all became clear to Rider. His facial expression smoothed out and sympathy replaced his annoyance. His arms dropped to his side. Even his stance loosened.

Yep.

He had seen it too. The inevitability of his relationship ending before it could even bloom into something permanent.

Then Rider surprised him by putting a hand on his shoulder, making him jolt in place. "She might love him. I'll give you that. Because they're close. They've been through a lot together. That's what happens. But dude," he squeezed his shoulder to get his point across, "she loves you too. I don't mean the kind she has for him. A different kind. Loving him doesn't take away how she cares about you."

But it felt like it did. She couldn't love two men. It wasn't possible.

"I don't agree with you."

Rider chuckled, letting go of his shoulder. "Don't let this asinine thinking ruin what good thing you have going on with her." Then he shot Junelle a look. "And stop putting these thoughts in his head. That's not helping either."

"I will protect my brother in any means necessary."

"Hey, I don't need you two arguing because of me. I..." He tossed a shoulder up, sighing. "Jake knows more about the case with Ivy than I do. She tells him more and I don't get anything. That shit pisses me off! I'm worried too! I want to help her too!"

He shoved a finger in his chest so hard with the last two statements, it jammed his finger, making him wince in pain. But whatever. That pain was much better than the one tearing him apart inside.

"Dude, you have it all wrong. Jo doesn't know shit. You know more than she does because your sister pried it out of me, and no doubt she tattled to you."

"Hey," Junelle scoffed, slapping Rider on the arm.

"I'm not wrong, sweetheart."

"Well, no, but still."

They shared a lovey-dovey look that made Jason want to puke. He settled for crossing his arms instead.

"I couldn't possibly know more than her."

"Yeah, you could. Because we didn't share anything with her today. She asked, we deflected. Because the shit we're finding out isn't going to help her."

"What else did you find out?"

He wasn't even sure he wanted Rider to answer that.

Rider shook his head, the sorrow leaking from his eyes. "Nothing, Jason. That's the problem. Her roommate was murdered and we got jack shit to report to her. No video evidence of this guy going in or out of the apartment. Fingerprints galore around the apartment that'll take forever to process. No evidence that's helpful from Ivy's body. And her room. Shit. Forensics will take forever getting back to us if they even find anything. They're so backlogged. This guy is like a ghost. I'm pissed I don't have anything useful to tell Jo. I'm ashamed. So I need you to get your head out of your ass and not screw this relationship up. Jo needs you. She doesn't need whatever shit this is right now."

Jason backed up a step when Rider moved closer. "Now get your ass back in that apartment and stop acting like you're on the verge of breaking up. Because you're not. And whatever stupid shit you're thinking that's going on between her and Jake, get it out of your head. Jake's too messed up to be thinking about anything like that. And Jo's not the kind of woman to lead someone on. You're insulting both of them for even thinking shit like that. Do you understand me?"

He swallowed hard. "Yeah. Thank you for putting me in my place. Rather than Jake."

Rider stepped back, laughing. "Dude, don't be so sure about that. That man might still be grieving, but he's got eyes like a hawk."

With that, Rider grabbed Junelle's hand and they walked away. Jason dragged his feet back inside the apartment, hoping and praying what Rider said was true. He liked his version rather than his sister's.

He locked the door and then looked around. Jake sat on the couch, but Victoria was nowhere to be seen.

"She went to your room." Jake tossed his head toward the open space next to him. "You might as well get comfortable here. I don't think she wants to talk to you right now."

What the hell did that mean?

To find out, Jason followed orders. There was even a beer waiting for him on the coffee table. He took a long swallow before looking at Jake.

"What did I do wrong that she doesn't want to talk to me?"

Jake fiddled with his bottle, silence dragging on for far longer than Jason liked. "We didn't hear everything out in the hallway, but we heard some. The part where you seem to think we know more about the case than we're letting on. How you're pissed at her about that."

Well, shit.

He'd gotten louder out there than he intended.

And he wasn't mad at Victoria. He had been hurt thinking she was keeping things from him. Shielding him, as if he couldn't handle those hard parts of her life. He might not be a cop like Jake, but he could handle the gruesome too. He would handle anything for her.

"I'm not mad—"

"Save your bullshit for someone else, Jason. I don't want to hear it. I gave my stamp of approval for you to her. Now I'm regretting that. You hurt her. I don't like anyone who hurts her."

Just another reason to assume they had more than friendly feelings for each other. One more nail in the coffin to his relationship.

"It wasn't my intention—"

"Again," Jake snarled, "I don't want to hear your bullshit. You were acting off the entire time we ate. Giving weird looks and shit. I don't know what's going on in your head, and I don't care. What Jo needs right now is support. Not more shit to worry about. So if you go in the bedroom tonight, I better not hear one tear. Because if you hurt her even more, you're going to see the side of me you've already gotten a glimpse of before. We both know that I let you take that gun from my hand. I could've easily kept it in my possession."

If you go in the bedroom tonight...

Not when. But if.

Was Jake telling him to get the hell out of his apartment?

To leave Victoria alone?

What the hell was even going on? How had things unraveled so quickly?

"I DON'T WANT you sparing my feelings. I need to know everything you know, Tate. Now."

Jo's hand trembled as she held the phone to her ear.

The moment she heard Jason shouting through the door, it all came crashing down on her. The way she was being held back from it all. No doubt because they wanted to protect her. Instead, it was causing problems everywhere she turned.

"Jo..."

"Damn it, Tate! Active investigation, my ass. Conflict of interest, my ass. Protocol, my ass! When have you ever let things like that get in your way. Treat me with the same courtesy and respect."

Tate sighed heavily in her ear. "The reason we haven't told you anything yet is because we don't *have* anything."

She slumped to the bed, her hand shaking even more.

"I'm sorry, Jo. I wish I had something to tell you. We're

not trying to keep anything from you. But do I think it's wise for you to work the case? No. I think you should take some time off and grieve your friend."

And let her mind wander? Imagine Ivy's last moments? Have her mind beat her up that she could've prevented all of this if only she would've caught the bastard already.

No.

She wasn't taking time off.

That would make the ache tearing her apart inside worse.

"I think you should go to hell," she spat. The moment the words came out, she regretted them.

That wasn't the kind of person she was. She didn't say things like that to the people who she respected and cared about.

Yet, he was holding her back. He was treating her like a defenseless woman. Like a child. He wouldn't hesitate to get right into the middle of things if it had been his roommate. So why did he think it was okay to keep her out of it?

"I deserve that."

He did. She wouldn't dispute it, yet an apology sat on the tip of her tongue. Except her mouth wouldn't move to spit it out.

"I'm worried about you, Jo."

"I never asked you to worry about me, Tate. I asked for the same courtesy you would ask of me."

Before she said anything she'd regret, she hung up.

Then she tossed her phone to the side.

She was done being treated this way. Messing up the case, especially when they caught the guy, wasn't what she was aiming for. She would stay out of it, but she wouldn't be pushed to the sidelines any longer.

Exiting the bedroom, her footsteps slowed as she neared the living room, hearing the heated exchange going on.

"I don't give a shit," Jake spat.

"Look, man—"

"Nope. Not listening to a word."

She sighed to announce her presence. Both men twisted around to look at her. "Someone want to tell me what's going on?"

Neither said a word.

"Jake?"

He flashed her a cocky smirk that she wanted to wipe off his face.

"Jason?"

He looked contrite. He shoved himself to a standing position and walked around the couch, but didn't come closer to her.

"I'm sorry you heard me hollering from the hallway."

Jake scoffed. "But not sorry for what you said."

"Look, asshole, I am. Which I was trying to say, but you kept interrupting me."

Jake sprung to his feet. "You're not sorry. You're only saying it because we heard it."

Jo walked around Jason, moving closer to Jake. Jason followed her movements, his expression morphing from annoyance to anguish in a blink of an eye.

"Why do you keep looking at me like that?"

Jason clenched his teeth, shaking his head. "Why did you walk around me and move closer to him?"

"What?"

What kind of question was that?

Jason let out a huge breath, his shoulders even slacking. "I thought you were keeping the case from me. I now know they've been keeping it from you. Not that they have much to share. I feel like I'm on the outside here. Maybe it's because I'm not law enforcement like everyone else. I see the way you two are with each other." Jason threw a hand back and forth, gesturing between her and Jake.

Jo glanced at Jake, who had cocked his brow at the statement, and returned her attention to Jason. Perhaps looking at Jake had been the wrong move. He appeared to be even more devastated.

"I don't understand what you're trying to say."

"I can't compete with that," Jason said in a tormented voice, his face scrunched in pain as he tossed a rigid hand at Jake.

Compete?

"Shit, dude. You're jealous." Jake laughed.

And this time when she looked at him, she threw in a nasty glare. It toned down his laughter, but didn't erase the smirk lining his face.

"Maybe I am." Jason sounded defeated. "Do you love him?"

She frowned. "Of course I do."

"That's what I thought."

Then, to her shock, Jason walked out of the room.

"What just happened?"

Jake cleared his throat, then sat back down, grabbing his beer. "Your boyfriend seems to think we want each other." Jake's brows rose as he leveled a hard stare at her. "And you solidified it by saying you love me."

"Yeah, idiot. Like a brother. Like I loved—" She sniffed as if that would hold back the tears she felt rising to the surface. Maybe it helped because none broke the barrier. Yet.

Jake shook his head, staring at the bottle in his hand. "I love you too, Jo. Like a sister. I will gladly step into Wally's place, as much as I wish I didn't have to. I want to pound in Jason's face right now for hurting you like this." He sighed, downing a large gulp before slamming it on the table. "But I am part of the problem. I got in his face when I shouldn't have. He's been nothing but kind to me since the moment I met him." Jake stood up. "I jumped to conclusions about the shit he was hollering about in the hallway. He's scared. Scared about this asshole who killed your roommate and he'll try something against you. Scared he's going to lose you to me. I can see why he thinks he's on the outside of things. I messed up."

"I'm scared too."

About so much, but she couldn't articulate it into words.

Jake moved closer and pulled her into a hug. "Not everyone can handle this job. I don't think Jason is one who can't."

She let go first, stepping away from him. "I need to go talk to him."

Jake nodded and resumed his position on the couch.

The door was closed when she ventured down the hallway. Though Jason had offered his place for her to stay, she didn't feel like it was her home or anything. Should she knock? Should she open it? A closed door spoke volumes.

Her knuckles met wood before she could change her mind.

"Jason? Can I come in?"

A muffled "yeah" echoed through the door.

She opened it to find him sitting on the edge of the bed. She took a spot next to him.

"Do you want me to leave?"

Victoria leaving was the last thing he wanted. But he wouldn't stop her if that's what *she* wanted.

He stared at her, trying to gauge what she was thinking. Nothing was easy to read. Despite the fear he'd already lost her, he reached for her hand and locked his fingers with hers.

"I don't want you to leave. But I'll accept it if that's what you want."

Her brows drew low, and he could see the wheels turning in her head as she processed something.

"Are you trying to push me away?"

He jerked at the question. "Absolutely not."

"Then why are we arguing? We don't argue with each other."

True statement. They rarely argued since they had started dating. Of course, they had the one time outside Jake's house. Emotions had been high. That one had seemed inevitable.

When she had to leave abruptly for work, he calmly said he understood. That was about the only thing he could think would cause any arguments between them. Because not everyone would put up with that. But he understood the mechanics of her job. How grueling it could be. The intricacies of it.

This argument also had been Jake as the cause. Why couldn't she see the correlation? What the problem was!

"I love you, Victoria. I've never said that to a woman before. The only thing I want is for you to be happy. If Jake makes you—"

"Jake is someone I will always love," she said, cutting him off at the same time she squeezed his hand hard, squishing his fingers to the point it hurt. "Like a brother. Nothing more than like a brother. I can't even say I've ever been attracted to him either. You either believe me or you don't. I will not be with someone who's going to question my friendship with someone I will not push out of my life."

"Considering I helped you get him back into your life, I would never make you push him back out."

She narrowed her eyes.

Because he hadn't confirmed he believed her.

He knew, without one inkling or doubt, how honest she was. If she said she loved him like a brother, he believed her.

"Forgive me." He lifted her hand, pressing a kiss to the back of it. "I'm an idiot. A stupid, jealous idiot. This is the last thing we should even be arguing about. You've lost someone important in your life, and I'm an asshole for making this about me."

She inclined her head slightly. He kissed her hand again, so damn grateful she was willing to forgive his idiocy.

"I don't like bringing work home. Don't expect me to want to talk about it. The moment I walk through the door, I want to leave it all behind." She leaned closer. "But if you ask something, I will always give you an honest answer, to a certain extent. I can't share some things with you. This thing with Ivy..." Her lips trembled. "I understand your anger at thinking you're being kept in the dark. I'm pissed too. They're treating me like a child and it's not right. I'm not a helpless woman."

Not one helpless bone in her body. He agreed. But the need to protect was strong. He understood where the other guys were coming from, even if she hated the idea.

Of course he didn't think it wise to voice that.

"Where do we go from here?"

Another question from her that threw him off. What did that mean?

He didn't want her going anywhere.

"I don't know."

The three words made her tremble.

They shook him to the core as well.

He answered in a way where he was saying he didn't know what she meant, but he should've articulated that better.

"I think I'm tired. I'm going to go to bed."

Going to bed and cuddling with her sounded like a solid plan, but the way she had said it made him think she didn't want him follow suit.

So he left the room, parting with a light kiss on her lips. He needed some sort of contact with her.

He took the same spot on the couch he had before, grabbing the unfinished beer bottle from the coffee table.

Jake had on the baseball game. For a while, neither spoke. They watched the game, letting the silence drag on.

"Why the hell are you out here and not with her?"

Jason flinched at the harshness in his tone. And a little from him breaking the silence. "It felt like she wanted space. I'm giving her what she wants."

"So you messed it up." Jake shook his head.

"I don't get you, man. You hate me or you don't?"

Jake sighed. "I like you despite also hating you at times." A cocky grin splintered his face. "If you can't take the heat, walk away. Because I'm never going to change. I will defend her in any way until my last breath. Because, as her honorary brother, that's what I do."

Jason laughed, tipping his beer toward him. "I can understand that. I'd defend Junelle to my dying breath as well."

A stiff nod answered him. "So, how'd you mess up in there?"

Jason shrugged. "I have no idea. We settled things

between us, which I thought was a good thing and then..." And then it took a sharp nosedive into confusion again. "She said she wanted to go to bed and it felt like she wanted to do that alone."

"You know what always messes up the relationships I'm in? My lack of communication." A sardonic laugh echoed between them. "My last girlfriend said I don't express my feelings enough. And it didn't bother me when she left." Jake's piercing stare made Jason want to look away but he didn't. "Maybe you think she wants to be alone, but seriously, dude. Should she be alone right now?"

No.

No, she should not be alone right now.

"You really confound me at times."

Jake's lips tilted into a shit-eating grin. "Always good to keep you on your toes."

He rolled his eyes, set his drink on the table, and stood up. "See you in the morning."

"Yep."

He used the bathroom first, grabbed two water bottles from the fridge, and closed the bedroom door behind him. Victoria was lying on her side, her back turned away from him. He made sure to be quiet as he set the bottles down and then took off his clothes, leaving his boxers on. If she had fallen asleep already, he didn't want to disturb her, so he eased into the bed without jostling it too much.

But he needed her to know he was here for her. He needed some sort of contact. The wide bridge gaining ground between them was unwelcome.

He slid under the covers and scooted closer to her, wrapping a light arm around her waist. She grabbed his hand, sliding her fingers with his.

"I didn't mean to wake you." But he was glad he didn't keep his distance.

"I wasn't sleeping." She squeezed his hand.

"I'm sorry for even leaving the room." He pressed a light kiss to her shoulder. "You asked where do we go from here and I responded with a stupid answer. I didn't know what it meant and I didn't know what to say."

The last thing he'd have happen was Victoria walking out on him because of his lack of communication. If she left, she'd be leaving with his heart on the floor for her to stomp all over it.

"If I had my way, you wouldn't even go back to your apartment—ever. You'd move in here. I'd buy you a ring. Ask you to marry me. We'd tie the knot. Talk about kids. Maybe have a few. Maybe have none. Grow old together and live a long, happy life. That's where I want to go from here." His lips met her shoulder once more, pressing harder. "But it's too much, too soon, and I don't want to scare you away."

She sighed but didn't say anything. Though her hand tightened around his, and he took that as a good sign. She wasn't shoving him away and telling him to knock it off.

The words were out and he couldn't take them back.

Nor did he want to.

She knew where he stood. The rest was up to her.

17

OH, boy!

The game was about to really amp up.

He couldn't wait to enact his next move. Detective Johansen had no idea what was coming her way. Picking the right moment would be key.

"I wish you would've taken the day off."

Yeah, well, he had things to do. A plan that needed to go off without a hitch. A little recon first, to make sure he made no mistakes.

"I'm sorry, sweetheart," he said with a sincere pouty face before kissing Tina on the lips. "I'll try and make it a half day. I promise."

Tina stretched, showing off her sweet, delectable body that he devoured last night. Trying to entice him for some more. They'd had a wonderful time with his sister and her stupid boyfriend celebrating the Fourth of July. It had been a long evening though. Tina had teased him throughout the entire party. The moment they got home, he punished her for her actions.

Tied her to the bed, whacking her with a whip.

She enjoyed every single second of it.

He took her once while tied up. Then another when he removed the bonds. And a third time because he couldn't help himself.

So the fact she was ready for round four should've been enough for him to call into work and feign sickness.

But it wasn't.

He had to have Detective Johansen for himself. To teach her a lesson. To describe in great detail the things he did to her roommate. To show her how pathetic she was. To laugh at all of them at their stupidity. Nothing would keep him at home.

"I'm going to hold you to that promise."

"How about this, sweetheart?" Then he picked up her hand, bringing it closer to the headboard. He tied the silk scarf to her wrist. Tight, where she wouldn't be able to escape, but not tight enough to leave marks. He straddled her body, picking up her other hand, tying that one as well.

"So you're not leaving quite yet." The desire in her eyes flared to life.

Oh, he was leaving.

The need clawing away at him was too powerful inside.

His lips pressed pebble-like kisses to her cheeks, down her neck, until he reached her ear.

"I'm leaving, Tina. You stay right here and wait for me. Just." He brushed his tongue across her nipple. "Like." Then he nibbled on the other nipple. "This."

"But—"

He grabbed her around the neck, squeezing. Not hard enough to restrict her air flow, but enough to show her who was in charge.

"You're my sweet girl. My obedient girl. You'll do as I say

without one word of protest." He lowered his mouth closer to her ear. "Do I make myself clear?"

"Yes." The whispered word sent a flash of desire to his cock.

It was a pity he didn't have time to ravish her body from head to toe. He could use the sex.

But as he got off the bed and stared at her, looking at her tied up, at his mercy, obeying his commands, it would make his return to her that much sweeter.

"Good girl, Tina."

Her eyes sparkled with desire.

With a touch of fear.

She was aroused, yet frightened at the turn of events.

This would be a good trial for her. To see if she would do for his future wife.

If she stayed quiet while he was gone, no reports from the neighbors about any noise, being the good girl he asked of her, she would pass the test.

He blew her a kiss and walked out of the room. He had somewhere to be. He wasn't sure what Detective Johansen's schedule looked like today, so getting to the precinct before she left was vital. She'd never know he was following her, gathering all the intel he could before he finally made his move.

"HOW WAS YOUR FOURTH OF JULY?"

Jo didn't look up from her computer at Rider's question. "Fine. And yours?"

"Yeah, fine."

He tried a few more times to engage her in conversation,

and every time she responded with as little words as possible. And with a short, clipped tone.

Three days had gone by.

Three days of no new leads.

Three days of all of them keeping her as far away from the case as possible, despite her constant badgering to be included.

She didn't care what they thought about her attitude. If they were going to keep her on the outside trying to look in, then she'd give them the same courtesy in return.

Footsteps echoed away from her desk.

"How long are you going to be like that with all of them?" Jake asked casually, as if he were asking about the weather.

"Until they stop treating me like a child."

"They're—"

She threw up a hand, halting the words that would prove he shared their views. Nothing else needed to be said. Jake knew that, closing his mouth.

While she appreciated his support, sticking around the city for as long as he was, she didn't need him joining ranks with everyone else.

"Jo?"

She looked away from her computer toward Jake. The sympathetic look on his face made her want to scream. It was too bad that sort of thing was unacceptable in public.

"Maybe we should take the day off. You've been working so hard these last few days and—"

"Is this what you and Jason were whispering about when I was in the bathroom this morning? You both looked guilty when I walked into the room."

He smoothed his expression out, leaving it blank. As if that would hide the truth from her.

"You both want me to step back. To take a day off. Then another. Then another. For how long? Until they catch her killer? Until I give up and stop bugging people about her case? Uh! Tell me."

Jake leaned closer, keeping his voice low. "You have not processed the fact Ivy is dead yet. You're doing what I did, but in the opposite way. I hid from the world. You're grabbing it by the balls and not letting go. Take a breather. Take a moment. Damn it, Jo! Cry or something."

Maybe she hadn't fully processed her grief. Maybe she didn't want to.

Staying busy kept the nasty images out of her mind.

Jason hadn't said anything, but she knew he knew the trouble she had sleeping. Tossing and turning. Sometimes even waking up in a cold sweat. Playing on her phone to distract her from thinking about Ivy.

Why should she cry? What would that solve? Would it make her feel better? Maybe in the moment, but it wouldn't sustain her throughout the day. Was she then supposed to cry all day, every day?

No. None of that sounded healthy to her, so she would continue to do what she was doing. Work, work, work.

"How long do you plan on staying?"

Jake jerked at the question, sitting back in his chair. "For as long as you need me."

"The couch can't be that comfortable."

A lackluster laugh spilled out. "I've slept in worst places, Jo."

"You should go home. You missed your interview. You need to get on with your life. Stop postponing your life because of me."

"I'm not postponing my life. I'm here because I want to be here. To help you."

"And how long do you think that will be?"

He grinned. "For as long as you need me."

She groaned, knowing this was a useless conversation. They would continue to go round and round in circles. She could say she didn't need him anymore and he'd disagree.

There was work to be done.

She stood up and Jake sprung to his feet too. Suppressing another groan was a challenge, but she did it.

"What happens if we never catch this guy?"

"Oh, we'll catch him."

The confidence was appreciated, but empty. Jake couldn't know for sure he'd be caught. Considering the lack of evidence, it was like looking for a needle in a haystack right now.

"So what were you and Jason talking about this morning?"

Jake shrugged. "What we're having for supper."

Her eyes narrowed as if that would scare him into telling her the truth.

"What Jason and I talked about is not a big deal. Don't worry about it."

But she would worry about it.

She'd been doing nothing but worrying about every aspect of her life since she came home from Minnesota. Things with Jason had turned a serious corner. For the most part, they had moved in together. Tate and Stromberg had gone to her apartment, bringing more clothes and toiletries to her. Even some of her books and movies. It wasn't a whole lot, but it was enough to say she had no intention of leaving anytime soon.

Moving in already? It was too fast.

Yet Jason's passionate speech the other night said

nothing was too fast for him. He'd jump to the alter if she said let's do it.

Now Jake was on her case about taking time off.

She didn't need more stress in her life. Work kept her sane and centered. Taking that away from her would be her downfall. She'd fall prey to the extreme grief that had hit Jake before they pulled him out of it.

"Whatever. I'm heading out. I got a phone call from someone saying they had information on the Stalton case."

A robbery that had left her victim in the hospital with a broken leg and fractured ribs. And he was out of an heirloom ring that was worth a quarter million dollars. She doubted she'd find the ring, but the person who left a message said they knew who took it. Maybe it was a lead, and maybe it wasn't.

"Who called?"

"They wouldn't give me a name. They were concerned about their safety."

Jake frowned, yet followed her.

"Don't look at me like that. I'm clearly not going alone to meet with some unknown person."

That garnered her a grin from him. "No, you aren't going alone."

"It's probably nothing. I get tips like this all the time that pan out to be nothing."

They walked outside. The sun was hot and already making her sweat as soon as the air hit her. No wind either, making it worse.

"Or it could be a trap?"

Her steps froze on the sidewalk.

Jake cocked a brow as if asking did she really not think about that?

To her amazement, she hadn't.

Would the killer be that brazen?

Would he target her next?

Well, of course he could. He'd left that disturbing message written in lipstick on the mirror. He'd been following her, keeping tabs on her life.

"So we're going in with our eyes wide open. Just because you pointed that out doesn't mean I'm not going to go."

"You worry me, Jo," Jake said, shaking his head, yet continued to follow her without further argument.

Yeah, and she worried that they'd never find the killer. If this was a trap...good! It would make taking him down that much easier—and sooner.

18

THE MORNING HAD BEEN DECENT. Despite the tense moment in the kitchen when he and Jake had some words with each other.

It had been such a stupid argument too. All over who was cooking supper that night.

He wanted to make steaks, but Jake insisted those could only be cooked on a grill. Yeah, well, when one lived in an apartment with no balcony, grilling was not an option.

Somehow the odd argument twisted and turned until the real issue came out.

What were they going to do about Victoria?

Jason didn't like how she was ignoring Ivy's death, working long hours, and not speaking about her. But he also understood she needed time to process her grief in her own way.

Jake didn't agree.

Of course he wouldn't.

Not when the man himself had fallen into his own dark pit of grief and barely made it out alive.

But whatever. Jason was giving Victoria some grace on everything because she'd been dealt a huge blow. Plus him coming on strong. The dynamics of their relationship turning so quickly. He couldn't rock the boat, no matter how much he wanted to side with Jake.

Jake wanted her to take the day off. A few days actually. They didn't even celebrate the Fourth yesterday. A case had come up, and Victoria worked well into the night. Of course, Jake stuck by her side. He had sat in the apartment by himself, worrying and wondering how she was doing.

Junelle had tried to get him to come over and he declined. He had wanted to be there for Victoria when she returned home. He had been. Yet, she took a bath, ate a quick meal, and crawled into bed. Though no sleep hit her. He wasn't an idiot. Sleep eluded her every night since she moved in.

All he wanted to do was be there for her, help her in any way he could, and half the time, he still felt like he was on the outside looking in.

Hell, Jake was with her more than he was. He'd gotten over his initial jealousy. Because Victoria had been correct. She wouldn't—and shouldn't—be with someone who didn't trust her. And he trusted that if she said there was nothing between the two, there was nothing between them.

He'd decided to work from home today. A bad habit forming, but he couldn't drag himself into the office.

The longer the morning wore on, the more his mind wandered.

Jake hadn't won the argument with Victoria to take the day off since they hadn't returned home yet.

The way she'd been pouring herself into her work, they wouldn't be home until late once again. Which made the silly argument about supper even more ridiculous. Anything he made would have to be heated up.

But he wanted to spend time with her. More than just in the bed where they lay silently together. But making love was the last thing she wanted to do. Of course, he understood why. Who could possibly be in the mood when they were surrounded by death and mayhem? Nobody!

Jason closed his laptop, set it on the coffee table, and stood up from the couch.

He'd surprise them at work. Take them for lunch. Have one meal with them for once. Feel like he was a part of her life, even when he felt so far on the outside of it.

It didn't take long to get to the precinct. A cop he recognized, but couldn't remember his name, manned the front desk.

Jerry, his name tag said on his uniform.

"Hi, Jerry."

He nodded, grunting an unintelligible greeting. Either because he wasn't a friendly guy or he couldn't remember who *he* was either, though recognized him.

"I'm here to see Detective Johansen."

Jason could've texted her—or even Jake—but he wanted it to be a surprise. Getting a call from the front desk was harder to turn him away than a text on the phone.

At least, he hoped so.

But would she turn him away?

Was he overstepping his boundaries?

Screwing up once more with her?

"I'm pretty sure she left with that other guy who's always lurking around her."

Jason chuckled. He doubted Jake would appreciate being described that way.

"Can you check?"

The man didn't look happy about the prospect, but picked up the phone anyway. Jason wandered over to the board where wanted posters were hanging alongside missing persons posters, and a whole variety of things. City bulletins. Public notices. A few newspaper articles from *The New York Chronicle* about some big cases getting solved.

Jason leaned closer, inspecting one of the photos attached to an article about a big drug bust that resulted in the arrest of a high-profile gang in the neighborhood. He removed it from the board, focusing on the guy with press credentials around his neck, standing next to two other people who looked like detectives, but it wasn't clear in the picture.

"Yeah, she left." Jerry scoffed. "What the hell are you doing? Put that back up."

He flinched at the outburst, curious about his irritation.

"I wanted a closer look at the article. Why is it hanging up?"

Jerry looked at him like he was an idiot. "Because that was a huge bust for the department. And I know the crime reporter. He had a hand in bringing down that gang. Good guy. I'm dating his sister. Why wouldn't I be proud of him?"

Well, Jason had an inkling there was one big reason not to be proud of him.

"Is Detective Rider in?"

Jerry groaned, grabbing the phone again. "Put that back up."

He would. As soon as he was finished with it.

Jason strolled over to the wanted posters where the sketch of their killer hung. He glanced at it, then at the newspaper article. Back and forth. Back and forth until his eyes blurred.

"He's in. You can go on back."

Jason smiled, then snatched the sketch off the wall too.

"Hey! I said to put that back up."

"Just borrowing it, Jerry. I'll hang it back up."

Then he walked away in a hurry before Jerry could stop him.

Rider was standing by Tate and Stromberg's desk when he walked into the large area where desks were scattered around the room.

"Hey, Jason. How's it going?" Stromberg asked, grinning up at him from his chair.

"Fine. Umm...so do you guys know this crime reporter in the photo?" Jason laid down the article, pointing at the picture where underneath it labeled the reporter as Chuck Moren.

Tate snorted in derision. "Unfortunately. Can't stand that asshole. He pokes his head into shit he doesn't belong in and half the time writes incorrect information."

"Why are you asking?" Rider asked, glancing at the article. "I remember that drug bust. Happened a few weeks ago. He was instrumental in bringing down the gang. Provided the detectives great intel on it."

Tate shifted in his seat. "My original comments stand as is."

Jason laid the sketch next to the article. "I've never met the guy. All I have is a grainy photo to work off of, but he bares a resemblance that I don't like."

All three detectives leaned in closer, inspecting both pieces of paper. Tate was the first to swear viciously, then stood up.

"I hate to say I agree."

Stromberg stood up as well. "Why do you hate to say that when you don't even like the guy?"

Tate's frown increased. "Because it points out how

horribly I missed the connection. Now that I've seen it, I can't unsee it. I can't wait to have a chat with him."

"He's a crime reporter. He's in here all the time. Talking to us, acting normal like he didn't brutally rape and murder women," Rider said in disbelief.

"There has also been a significant lack of evidence at both crime scenes. This killer knows how to avoid the cameras. He's smart." Stromberg paused. "As if he knows how crime scenes work. As if he knows what the police will look for."

"Shit." Rider pulled out his phone. "I'll call Jo, see where she's at. I know her and Jake went to check out a witness statement or something. Chuck is always milling around, popping up at various crimes scenes. No wonder he knew how you started dating her."

A chill swept across his body.

Victoria had been in close proximity to this killer on multiple occasions and never even knew it.

"Do you think she's in danger?" God, Jason hoped not.

"No, but I'm done keeping her in the dark." Rider stared hard at Tate and Stromberg as if daring them to argue with him. "She has a right to know our suspicions. And to be wary if Chuck shows up where she's at."

"WELL, that was a complete waste of our time. The dude was the biggest moron I've ever met and I'm pretty sure he's in a bad need for a fix," Jake commented as they walked through the abandoned warehouse where her witness wanted to meet.

Her nerves were wrought from Jake putting in her head this could've been a setup by the killer.

And it hadn't been.

The guy had been legit. Though, as Jake said, a complete waste of time. He'd seen the robbery take place, but he'd been high as a kite. Anything he told her would be rocky in court. He was a far cry from a reliable witness. Plus, he couldn't provide much of a description of the perpetrator. Jo was pretty sure the guy was hoping to get a small reward in the form of money for his horrible information so he could get high once again.

She refused to play his game. Until he had better information, like a name or even a semi-description of the guy, she wasn't giving him anything.

Right now, all he could say was the guy had on clothes. Dark clothes, to be specific. That was it. No facial descriptions. Not what *kind* of clothes he wore. She figured he could've been a little better at faking it if he wanted some money.

But he was looking worse for the wear, so he wasn't in the right frame of mind.

The closer they got to the exit, the more her nerves settled.

Even a smile appeared.

"What are you smiling about?"

She bumped shoulders with him. "Because you had my insides all up in knots and...well, this was nothing. I feel bad for the guy. I wish he would've accepted my offer of help."

It hadn't been much.

She suggested he go to the nearest shelter. Get some food, a good night's sleep. The stench coming off him with the look of his clothes said the guy was living on the streets. She offered to bring him there. Get him set up. Make sure he had a bed.

He spit in her direction, missing her by inches, and stormed off.

"Not everyone wants that kind of help."

"Yeah, I know."

Her phone rang, piercing the quietness surrounding them. She even jumped a little at the noise.

"It's Rider," she said, glancing at the screen. "Hey, what's up?"

She listened to his quick rundown of what transpired, her nerves reappearing and sending chills up and down her spine.

"Chuck Moren? I can't even believe it. Thanks for the info. I'll relay it to Jake. We're on our way back to the precinct. My witness didn't pan out."

The phone vanished inside her pocket and they resumed walking.

"Well? What's up?"

So many things, and she didn't know where to start. To think she spoke to the man. Many, many times. It was unfathomable to believe Chuck Moren was the rapist and killer, and yet, when her mind conjured an image of him, she didn't doubt it at all. It was so obvious now that it'd been said out loud.

The asshole had even come to her apartment building the night she found Ivy.

Another shiver wracked her body.

He pretended as if he knew nothing about what happened.

Looked right into her eyes, feigning innocence when he'd been the one to strip Ivy's life away.

"Jo?"

She was in a daze as they walked, realizing she'd never answered Jake's question. Before she could, a dark shadow appeared from the side, swinging something heavy toward Jake, making contact with his head.

Jake crumbled to the ground without even one moan or cry of surprise. Jo even watched as a small pool of blood emerged on the concrete.

Her entire body froze, her mind disjointed as she watched the shadow move closer into the light.

Even though her gut had confirmed Rider's suspicions, the truth stood in front of her.

Chuck laughed, gripping the large pipe in his hand. No doubt he'd picked it up from somewhere in the building.

"It's you and I now, detective."

And she knew exactly what he wanted to do.

The same thing he'd done to the first victim, Rowena. The same thing he'd done to Ivy. Jo knew, the same thing he had done to countless other women.

"Why are you doing this?"

Maniacal laughter fell out of his lips. "This is not the part where I confess all my sins. So asking questions is pointless. Though, I have a few questions. Who called you? And why was I a part of the conversation?"

Ha!

Like she'd answer his questions when he wouldn't answer hers.

The door to the outside world stood about twenty feet away. She didn't want to leave Jake, but there was nothing she could do for him right now. Getting far away and some help had to be her priority. If she could make her feet move. If she could get her body to reconnect with her mind.

Her gun was strapped to her waist, with her phone in her pocket. Grabbing for her phone would take too long. He'd attack before she could even unlock it to make a call.

She could reach for her gun, but he stood too close. Getting off a shot would be iffy.

But she had to keep him talking until she decided her next plan of attack.

"We know everything, Chuck. The game is over for you. Wouldn't your best bet be to leave the city? Get away before everyone closes in on you."

"But I didn't confess anything to you. What do you think you know? You can't tie me to any crimes. There's no evidence to say I did anything wrong."

She waved a hand toward Jake, though didn't look at him. She'd lose the tiny thread of bravery she had left in her. Because her nerves were threatening to overwhelm her.

"You hit my friend over the head. You have now committed a crime. An assault."

Chuck tossed the pipe back and forth in his hands. "Yeah, but you won't live to tell anyone it was me. And if your friend survives, he didn't see anything. Therefore, he can't give a description of me."

His confidence wasn't surprising. Though, sometimes that could be a person's disadvantage, especially for someone like him. Overconfidence could create mistakes. Could bring down their guard, thinking they're safe.

"My friends will make sure you rot in prison. I can guarantee that."

"No, I don't think so. They have nothing to tie me to anything."

"The sketch. We have that."

He chuckled again. "That's so generic. Do you know how long that's been hanging up there?" More laughter escaped. "Of course you do. You hung it up. Jerry's dating my sister. The guy has had it next to him the entire time and he's never even connected the dots. It won't stand in the courtroom. It's not enough to convict me for anything."

She would take that as a confession, more or less.

Yep. Too much overconfidence.

Jerry?

Front desk Jerry?

She could only assume that's who he was talking about, but she wasn't going to ask for confirmation.

"Do you think I'm going to let you hurt me? Do what you did to Rowena? To Ivy!"

"Oh, my sweet detective, I'm hoping you don't let me. Because the fighting is the best part."

This man was certifiable.

If she didn't do something to get herself out of this, he would kill her. She knew how to protect herself, but she wasn't naive to think she was stronger than him. If he got the upper hand—and he likely could—she was a goner.

"Did you know the national animal for Scotland is the unicorn?"

He flashed a look of surprise. "What?"

"When it comes to an octopus, they have three hearts, their blood is blue, and nine brains. Nine!"

The puzzlement continued to invade his face.

"If you're going to keep any kind of food in the house, you should have honey. It never spoils." Then she jerked her attention to the left, widening her eyes. "You're finally here!"

Chuck also looked in the direction of her exclamation.

It was enough time to pull her weapon out and aim it at him.

Again, overconfidence.

Nothing like a bit of random facts to jumble a person's focus and then direct their attention somewhere else.

She wished someone had actually arrived, but no one was coming to her rescue. She had to do this all on her own.

"Put down the pipe and put your hands against the wall over there. You're under arrest."

Instead of complying, he smirked. "You won't shoot me."

"Despite you thinking you know me, Chuck, you have no clue what I'm capable of." She didn't know what she was capable of either until this moment. Because if she had to pull the trigger, she would.

19

"Oh, my sweet detective. I know you won't shoot me. You're not that kind of person."

If this man called her his sweet detective one more time, she'd shoot him for that reason alone.

"Do as I say now. You're under arrest."

"For what charges?"

Wow. Did she have to spell it out?

Or maybe this was his way of distracting her.

Yes.

That's what he was doing. Trying to get her off-balance as she had done to him.

"Here's the thing, Chuck. My friend is knocked out cold. There's no one else around. No witnesses. Nobody to know why I shot you. You hurt my friend here. You killed my roommate. You pretended to be a good guy when you're nothing more than a disgusting rapist and murderer. I have no qualms about shooting you. So unless you want to be wheeled out of this place in a body bag, I suggest you follow my directions and put your hands on the wall."

The cracks in his armor were starting to appear. The

slightest spark of fear hit his eyes. Her words were making an entrance. The belief was becoming real.

"You know what your problem is, Chuck? You thought you were invisible. You thought you were untouchable. You thought you were smarter than everyone else around you. And truth is, you're none of those things. You're a weak, sorry excuse for a man. I think deep down you know that."

His joyful attitude vanished, replaced by fury. His eyes jolted with anger, as his hand tightened around the pipe.

This time, he doled out the surprise, tossing the pipe in her direction. She had to move out of the way, moving her aim. At the same time, he leaped at her. She didn't drop the gun as he made contact, but she hit her head hard on the concrete. His body covered hers, pinning her to the ground. Then his hand wrapped hers holding the gun.

If he got the gun out of her hands, she was a goner.

"Give up, detective. You had a nice try there, but it's over. I always win. Because pathetic people like you never have a chance against me."

They struggled with the gun, her grip on it as tight as could be. She would not give up her only means of surviving. He tried twisting it out of her hands.

With one hand groping for the weapon, he used his other hand to smash her head against the concrete. Stars danced before eyes. Bells rang in her ears. But the hold on her lifeline did not lessen.

The gun twisted this way and that way.

The evil, sadistic way he stared at her while fighting for the gun made her sick to her stomach. Despite not overpowering her yet, he was enjoying this moment. She could even feel him growing hard as she lay beneath him.

Disgusting, evil man.

Then a loud, cracking sound echoed in the building as

Jake swung the pipe hard at Chuck's head. He tumbled to the side, eyes closed, unconscious from the blow. Just as blood had poured from Jake's wound, the same happened to Chuck. Pooled underneath his head, coating his hair and the concrete surrounding him.

She scooted away, the gun still firmly in her hand until she met resistance.

Jake's body.

His arms wrapped around her, holding her tight.

"You okay?"

She brushed a light hand across his cheek, smearing some of the blood. "Better than you. I thought...I thought for a moment..."

"Shh...Jo. It's going to take more than a pipe to the head to kill me off. I'm okay."

"Cuff him please."

Because the way her hands were shaking, she knew it would take too long for her to get the job done.

Jake took the cuffs she held in her hand and did it without batting an eye. Chuck made no sound as Jake jostled him.

"Don't worry, he's not dead. He's still breathing."

She didn't know how she felt about that. It wouldn't have saddened her if the blow had killed him.

"He killed Ivy."

Jake sat down by her, putting an arm around her. "Yeah, I know. I figured that out pretty quickly when I came to and saw him straddling you."

"He was..." She swallowed, not even sure she could voice any of it. Yet, if she didn't say it now, she might not ever speak of it. "He was getting off on what he was doing to me. I could feel...his arousal."

Jake's hold strengthened around her. "It's over now. He

can't hurt you again. I know that if I hadn't stepped in, you would've handled it fine."

She wanted to believe that. Oh, how she wanted to believe that.

But she wouldn't have kept ahold of the gun for too much longer. The man's strength couldn't be denied.

"I'm glad you're here, Jake."

"Shit, Jo. Me too." Then he kissed the side of her head, hugging her tighter. "We should call the calvary."

"Yeah. Of course."

Except, in the end, she couldn't find her voice yet. Jake called Rider.

Police and EMT services arrived and things happened in such a hurry. Chuck was loaded into an ambulance and went on his way. She also needed to go the hospital along with Jake. He needed stitches and she needed a few of her own. When Chuck had launched himself at her, she'd hit her head hard enough to make a small crack in her skull. Nothing where it bled like Jake's had, but enough where she needed a stitch or two.

She didn't even remember the ride to the hospital. All her mind kept doing was going through the events of the day.

What she could've done differently. What could've happened if Jake hadn't woken up.

And where did she go from here?

JASON SAT in Victoria's work chair, unsure of what to do. Did he leave? Did he wait? Did he continue to go out of his mind with worry? Or trust the fact that Victoria could handle herself and her co-workers had her back?

Because he stood by while Rider called her. Told her everything they were suspicious of. Rider ended the call and said Jo and Jake were on their way back to the precinct. In the meantime, those three left to find Chuck.

And he was left with nothing to do but wait.

As much as he wanted to join the guys, he couldn't. He wasn't a cop. While Jake wasn't a cop in New York, he had carried a badge in Minnesota. Jason wasn't sure how he was allowed to come to work every day with Victoria. He assumed he'd worked something out with her boss.

Time passed by as slow as molasses as he waited. And waited. And waited.

Where was she? How long would it take from wherever she was to return to the precinct? Would she even want him here?

Maybe he should leave.

"Hey, Jason."

He looked up, spacing out from his wandering thoughts, to see Detective Sterling.

"Hi. I was..." Leaving? Staying? What the hell was he doing?

Detective Sterling offered a gentle grin, then gestured his head toward the exit.

So he was being asked to leave. Got it.

"You can ride with me to the hospital."

He jumped to his feet. "What do you mean?"

Detective Sterling motioned his hands up and down, telling him to calm down. "Everything is fine. But Jo and Jake needed to get a few stitches. They caught the guy. Chuck. It's over." Maybe the panic was written all over his face because the detective reached out, guiding him to leave. "It's fine. They're fine. Like I said, just a few stitches."

Well, he wouldn't believe it until he saw it with his own eyes.

The ride to the hospital felt like it took ages.

Rider was in the lobby when they arrived, taking over for Sterling, and led him to where Victoria was.

"Look." Rider stopped outside the door to her room. "She's fine. But she's out of it. He attacked her. Okay. He was on top of her and...I don't think she's processed it yet. Don't..."

Don't, what?

What would he do? What the hell did Rider think he would do?

"Don't come on strong."

Meaning he had been coming on too strong with her.

Got it.

All the worries that had been plaguing him were not unfounded. They were real and serious and he was so out of his depths when it came to having a relationship with someone like Victoria.

"I got it."

Then he shoved past Rider and into the room.

Victoria smiled at him, but no light shined from her eyes. She looked exhausted. Yet he didn't see evidence of any injuries.

"A few stitches on the side of my head." She touched the right side of her head. "It's no big deal. It was only two. Jake had to have ten."

Geez.

That was a lot.

While he wanted the whole story, he didn't say a word as he sat down next to the bed and held out his hand. She interlocked her fingers with his, sighing. If he had to guess, in relief. That he hadn't bombarded her with questions.

They sat in silence, though there was a flurry of activity in the room. Cops in and out. Rider with Tate and Stromberg at times. People asking Victoria questions. The nurses popping in on occasion.

Throughout it all, Jason understood what was going on without asking any questions of his own.

Chuck had hit Jake over the head, knocking him out. Victoria had done her best to get out of the situation by herself, but somehow Chuck overpowered her and tried to get her gun. She put up a helluva fight. Jake swooped in as her savior, returning the favor with the pipe.

They found Chuck's girlfriend tied to his bed, naked. The woman wasn't giving a clear picture of why Chuck had done that. Had she been his next intended victim?

They were combing his apartment, hoping to find some small shred of evidence to tie him to the crime scenes. Because he had never confessed to Victoria about hurting anyone.

The notion he could get away with it all pissed Jason off so much, he found himself squeezing her hand hard more times than he liked. Every time, she looked at him funny but didn't say a word.

He figured she knew where his anger and frustration were coming from because no doubt she felt the same way.

Some time later, Jason wasn't even sure how much later, Jake strolled into the room. He looked as tired as Victoria. Too much blood on his clothes as well.

"Doc's discharged me and you're free to go as well. Let's go home."

He didn't need to be told twice.

Though, he hadn't driven here so he had no means to bring these two home. They got a ride from another officer.

Victoria let Jake use the shower first. Still not much was said between them until it was her turn to clean up.

Jake took a seat next to him on the couch.

"How bad was it?" He hated to ask, but if he was going to ask anyone, it had to be Jake over Victoria.

"Pretty bad. It could take time for her to get through it."

He had all the time in the world. She already knew where he stood in the relationship. He was in it for the long haul. Until death do us part.

"So you're sticking around some more?"

Jake grinned, shaking his head. "I think you can handle the rest. It's time for me to get through my own shit."

"You're welcome here anytime, Jake."

"That's why I'm leaving without any worries. Because I know Jo's in good hands with you."

Victoria came out of the bathroom a while later, but didn't join them in the living room. While Jason didn't want to bother her, he also didn't want to leave her alone to her thoughts. He knew they'd wander to parts they shouldn't. At least, not yet.

He found her curled up in the bed. Hesitation hit him, then he got over it and climbed into bed with her.

She grabbed his arm after he draped it across her, squeezing so hard, her fingernails dug into his skin.

"I'm here for whatever you need from me. I love you, Victoria."

"I know you do."

Jason didn't know why those simple words bothered him, but the worry he'd experienced earlier spread throughout his body once more.

20

THE LAST TWO days had been surreal. She felt like she had been floating on a cloud, looking down at everything going on around her.

"Detective Johansen, are you listening?"

Trying to, but failing miserably.

She cleared her throat, offering a weak smile to her captain. "Yes, sir."

"I want you to take some time off."

"But sir—"

He held up his hand for her to stop. She complied right away. The fight in her wasn't strong anyway.

"I know you haven't been handling the investigation concerning your roommate, which is a good thing. Conflict of interest and all that. But you've been around the last two days while they tie all the loose ends together."

She had been.

Lingering outside Chuck's hospital room while they interrogated him. The asshole wasn't speaking. Claiming he'd been attacked by them for no reason.

His girlfriend, who had been tied to his bed, said they

liked rough, unusual sex. Believable for some couples, but Jo knew better. Chuck was a perverted, sick man. He would've eventually hurt his girlfriend like he hurt Rowena and Ivy. Of course, she'd been horrified when they told her everything he was being accused of. She left him.

His sister stood by his side, not believing a word of the alleged crimes against him. Though Jerry, he believed the cops over his girlfriend and broke up with her.

The Moren siblings were on their own in their beliefs. Victoria figured the sister was in denial more than anything. It had to be hard to imagine your brother could do such unspeakable things. She would know. Sometimes, even she couldn't believe her brother, Wally, had killed his wife, her lover, and a mother accused of abuse. She sympathized with May Moren. She knew the struggles the woman was going through.

"But you're not all here. You're distracted. You were attacked. You almost died. Your roommate was murdered. You need to take time. It's something I should've insisted from the beginning. You can't return until you're cleared by the department psychologist. Am I clear?"

Crystal.

But it didn't mean she liked it.

It also didn't mean she didn't understand it.

She knew she needed the time to process it all. But it was so hard to stand back and let others handle it. She wanted to beat a confession out of him. Demand answers. Why would he hurt those women? Why fixate on her? What had been his end game by killing her?

"Detective Johansen? Do I make myself clear?"

She cleared her throat again, nodding. "Yes, sir."

"Go home."

She stood up and left the room. Then the precinct.

Without stopping to chat with anyone, though many looked at her as if they had questions she had no answers for.

Standing on the sidewalk outside the precinct, she wondered where was her home? Her apartment where violent memories would attack her? Or Jason's where her conflicted emotions would make her go out of her mind?

Jason had been nothing but supportive through it all. Jake's problems. Ivy's death. The capture of her killer. The last two days he'd been by her side, making sure she was okay in every single way.

She knew he loved her. That he wanted a forever kind of life with her.

But she was nowhere ready for that.

Not yet at least.

Her captain was right. She needed to take time to herself.

The decision was clear.

She went to Jason's first and packed up all her belongings. He wasn't home and she wasn't sure if she was grateful for that or not. He deserved a reason for her leaving, but part of her was thankful he wasn't there.

A letter would have to suffice.

Jason,
Maybe this won't come as a surprise, but I need time to myself. So much has happened lately and my mind is a jumbled mess. You have no idea how much your support has meant to me. I know I wouldn't have made it through it all without you by my side, especially the hard issues concerning Jake. I am forever in your debt that you helped him back to the living world. That you invited him into your life, into your apartment. It's one of the reasons I love you. Don't think that because I'm leaving that it means I don't love you. I do. I really, really do. I need to sort

things in my life and I have to do it alone. I hope you understand.

Don't give up on me.
With love,
Victoria

She placed the note on his kitchen counter and hesitated to leave.

Life could be wonderful here. A partner to help her through her turmoil. Nights with someone who understood her. A man who supported her in every way.

Yet, staying also frightened her. That she wouldn't be able to move on without facing her demons on her own.

There were so many she had to confront.

She left before she chickened out and returned to her apartment.

The air was thick and musty, indicating it had been vacant too long of human life.

The first thing she did was empty out the refrigerator and buy new groceries. A person had to eat to survive.

Then she put her movies and books back in their place and tidied up the living room and kitchen. The bathroom wasn't too messy, but she cleaned that anyway.

Next she returned her clothes to the closet and the dresser drawers. She washed her sheets and remade her bed.

The closed door at the end of the hallway made her heart rate pick up in speed as she stared at it.

One room left to tackle.

Yet, she wasn't ready to enter Ivy's room.

She found herself leaving her apartment and heading to the hospital. Chuck would be released tomorrow and making his new home in a jail cell. If they couldn't find anything to connect him to the murders, he'd at least go to prison for attacking her and Jake.

Rider was at the hospital when she got there. By the tortured look on his face, he knew that she'd left Jason. Which meant Jason also knew. Yet, he hadn't called her. He hadn't reached out to change her mind. Even in this, he supported her and her decisions.

"Hi, Jo."

"He confess yet?"

Rider shook his head. "I hear you moved back home."

She nodded.

"Let me know if you need anything. Junelle and I are here for you."

But no mention of Jason. Kind of odd, yet he probably didn't want to get in the middle of it.

"He can't get away with this."

"He won't, Jo. We're going through his life with a fine-tooth comb. He's not providing alibis for either murder, but we're interviewing everyone he knows, trying to pin him down. We'll get him for both murders. I promise you. I hear the captain asked you to take some time off."

Well, hasn't he been hearing a whole lot lately?

"He did."

"Then do that. You shouldn't be here."

Ouch.

Not that he was wrong.

"Have Ivy's parents said anything about...her belongings?"

The sadness in Rider's eyes hit Jo in the gut. He didn't even need to voice it out loud.

"No. When we spoke to them, notifying them of her

death, they said thanks and then shut the door on our faces."

No surprise there. Ivy had spoken openly about the disdain her parents had for her and her lifestyle. That they'd cut her out of their lives years ago. They were very religious and Ivy didn't even believe in God. Realizing that made it even harder to deal with.

"And what about her...funeral arrangements?"

Rider shrugged. "They haven't claimed her body or anything. And you know what happens when no one claims a body."

She did. They went to Hart Island, where people went when their bodies were either unclaimed or unidentified.

But Ivy had people who cared about her. She cared about her.

"Then I'll handle the arrangements. She deserves a proper send off."

Rider smiled, bowing his head in understanding. "You're a good person, Jo. I think Ivy would like knowing you're the one handling it and not her parents."

She liked to think so.

Then she turned around to leave.

"Jason's a good guy too. I know you have your reasons for leaving. I like to think that the last part in your letter meant you aren't leaving for good."

Her back was to him. She couldn't even turn around as she replied. "I hope it is, but I don't know, Rider. I don't know."

Then she walked away to try and get her life back on track.

21

One month later

"You hear that? That's the beautiful sizzle of a steak being cooked on the stove. Wish you could smell it. Your mouth would be watering like mine is right now."

Jake chuckled in his ear. "Dude, come visit me soon and I will cook you a proper steak. I feel sorry for you right now."

"Whatever, man."

Jason had to admit he felt sorry for himself as well. But not about steaks.

He'd been the one to reach out to Jake first three weeks ago. After a whole week of not hearing from Victoria, he couldn't handle the silence. He'd respected her wishes about needing time to herself. He didn't call. He didn't text. He gave her the space she had asked for.

It didn't mean he wasn't going out of his mind with worry. So much anxiety that he'd lost a few pounds.

When he first called Jake, he'd lost his voice. Stumbled on his words, trying to articulate why he even called. But

Jake just knew. Because Victoria hadn't been ignoring Jake. Not like she'd cut off communication with him.

While Jake couldn't offer many answers about when she'd be back in his life, he'd settled some of the concern for him. She was doing okay. She was working through the horrors that had touched her life. Like he was day by day.

Since that day three weeks ago when he called, they'd kept in contact. Calling each other every other day, chatting. Sometimes texting.

It was his lifeline to Victoria, and he needed it like he needed his next breath. Not even Rider had contact with her. Once she left the precinct for time off, she didn't return. She didn't talk with anyone there.

Though that didn't mean Rider didn't provide him with updates about Chuck and sealing the deal for a solid conviction in the murders. They were still building a case against him. Still trying to place him at the locations of the crimes. They were making headway, poking holes in his alibis he finally supplied. And, lucky for them, they managed to find a fingerprint on the fire escape to Victoria's apartment. That wouldn't be there if he hadn't broken in and killed her roommate.

"How's the project going? Nearly done, right?"

The apartment building they'd been renovating when a killer tainted the scene. Yes, it was almost done. He couldn't wait to never see that place ever again.

"We'll be finished by the end of the week. I can't wait to say goodbye to it." He flipped the steaks, inhaling the wonderful aroma. This shit would be delicious, no matter what Jake thought about it being cooked on the stove. "And you? How's Neptune treating you? Anything crazy happen this week?"

"No, thank God. I like this small town. I like the petty

squabbles the people have. The non-violent crimes I deal with every day. I've started walking to work. It's a few blocks from my house. I grab coffee at the local cafe every morning. I'm trying to put myself out there. Get to know the townsfolk. It's not easy. It's...a different approach for me."

"Good for you, man. You got this. One day at a time."

"Yeah. One day at a time."

The heavy sigh Jake released told Jason that that wasn't always easy. He knew firsthand how difficult it was. He did the same thing when it came to Victoria. One day at a time. Every morning he woke up hoping that day would be the day she came back into his life.

A knock sounded on his door.

"Yo, man, I have to go. Someone's at the door."

"Enjoy those mediocre steaks. Talk to you later."

He removed the pan from the stove and turned the burner off. Then he jaunted to the door and opened it.

It's as if his thoughts—though they were constant—had conjured the one person he'd been dying to see since the day she left.

Victoria stood with a nervous smile, but with hope in her eyes.

"Hi."

"Hey."

They both laughed as they greeted each other at the same time.

"Come in." He waved her in. "I made steak. Are you hungry? Do you want to eat?" What was he doing? Jumping right into the notion she was staying for a while. "Or maybe not. Did you—"

She laid a hand on his arm, quieting his rambling. "I'd love to stay for supper. It smells delicious."

He gestured for her to take a seat and grabbed two

plates, filling them with steak, a baked potato, and corn, and delivering it to the table. He wished he had rolls of some kind but tried not to worry too much about it. Victoria showing up had been the last thing he expected.

They ate in silence, clearing their plates before coming to the reason for her appearance.

"I'm sorry, Jason."

For what? Leaving him? That she didn't want to continue a relationship? That she was about to break his heart?

"I didn't mean to leave the way I did."

"I'm not mad. I get it."

Her brows drew low. "I know you do. Sometimes, I wonder why I left the way I did when you're so understanding."

"You don't have to explain yourself, Victoria. You were going through a lot. I mean, still are."

"No." She reached out her hand across the table. "I've come to terms with it."

Had she? In one month? That fast?

But who was he to question her about her own feelings. His hand connected with hers. She squeezed it.

"Thank you for the flowers you sent to Ivy's funeral. I thought you'd show up."

"I wanted to, but I also didn't want to invade your space."

"I get to return to work next week. The captain gave the okay. It hasn't been that bad talking to someone about everything. I told Jake he should do the same thing."

Jason doubted Jake would. That wasn't his way of dealing with things. But Jason was glad Victoria had found it helpful.

"I'm happy to hear that."

She leaned closer, gripping his hand harder. "Did I ruin

things between us? Was I away too long? Do you still love me?"

He repositioned their hands so they were holding each other by the wrists, feeling their heartbeats. Both were beating wild...and in tune.

"They say that the heartbeats of two people synchronize when they're in love."

Wetness pooled in her eyes, a tear or two escaping as a smile broke free on her face. "I do love you. So much it hurt to be away from you. Yet, I needed that time to face it all by myself. I'm sorry if I hurt you in the process."

"I won't say I wasn't hurt by you leaving because that would be a lie. It killed me every day to wake up and not reach out, not check on you. Offer my help in some way. But you're here now. I didn't give up on you. So I'm hoping that your presence here means that you haven't given up on us."

"Never."

They stood up at the same time, colliding into each other's arms. The kiss they shared was one filled with passion, anger, pain, and forgiveness all rolled into one. It was fierce and so intense that when they broke apart, their heavy breaths were the only sound to fill the room.

"My lease is up on my apartment. Well, I asked to be released from it. They were pretty understanding why."

He couldn't stop the grin from forming. "So you need a new place to live?"

She bit her bottom lip as her own smile couldn't be stopped. "I was wondering if you knew a good place I could find."

"Yeah, I know of one." His heart filled with immense joy. "Do you want a tour of it? I'll show you right now."

She nodded, shrieking in delight when he picked her up.

He peppered kisses on her neck, her cheeks, and her lips as he carried her to the bedroom.

He gently laid her on the bed, kissing her with the utmost tenderness. "This is the bedroom. It's my favorite place in the apartment, but only when you're in it as well."

"It's a very nice bedroom. A big closet too. All my clothes will fit." She smoothed her hands through his hair. "So you forgive me?"

"There's nothing to forgive. But next time, if you feel the need to leave, say it to my face. Not through a letter. I think that hurt the most."

"There will not be a next time. You said that you were in this for the long haul. Through marriage and babies—if we want them—until we grow old together and die. Me too. I want all of that too. It doesn't mean it will be easy. My job is demanding and I'll miss things I will hate to miss."

"I'm going in with my eyes wide open. I know what a life with you will be like, Victoria. I'm ready to start living it."

Then he sealed those words with the touch of his hands to show her how much he loved her.

TO FIND OUT HOW ABBY & TATE MET, START DARK CONSEQUENCES TODAY!

For Tate & Abby's story

Dark Consequences

A Consequences Novel, #1

Every choice has a consequence...

Detective Tate Powell lives for one thing: revenge against the man who killed his sister. But when he discovers that man is none other than his girlfriend Abby's brother, his world shatters.

Torn between loyalty to her troubled brother and her feelings for Tate, Abby faces an impossible choice. She must betray the man she loves to protect her family. Even if it means turning against Tate forever.

As Tate's thirst for vengeance spirals out of control, he risks losing Abby and damning his own soul. Will he choose retribution or redemption before he loses Abby forever?

With gut-wrenching twists and taut suspense, this gripping thriller will leave romantic suspense fans on the edge of their seats. Find out in the explosive first book of the Consequences series!

For Wyatt & Brielle's story

Cruel Consequences

A Consequences Novel, #2

Some consequences can be so...cruel.

Working cold cases never bothered Detective Wyatt Stromberg—until one unimaginably brutal murder that haunts his dreams. Finding closure for the victim's sister Briella becomes an obsession. She's equally tormented by guilt that she failed her sister and is determined to ensure the killer faces justice.

As they grow dangerously close to the truth, and each other, the killer resurfaces, and he has his sights on Briella. Why now? Why allow a year to pass first? It doesn't matter—Wyatt vows to protect Briella no matter what. But the killer's sinister game of cat-and-mouse lurks around every corner, testing Wyatt's limits.

To save Briella, Wyatt must walk a tightrope between breaking protocol and breaking the law. With lives on the line, can he toe that precarious line before the killer checkmates them all?

With harrowing twists and turns, this gripping thriller will leave romantic suspense fans on the edge of their seats. Don't miss the next intense book in the Consequences series!

For Rider & Junelle's story

Fatal Consequences

A Consequences Novel, #3

One decision can have fatal consequences...

Detective Rider's life is spiraling. After nearly dying in the line of duty, now he's saddled with two babysitters as partners and an attitude problem his captain won't let slide. Just when he thinks his luck can't get any worse, he's thrown a case involving a woman who shattered his heart years ago—and the best friend he was forced to leave behind.

Junelle Swanson thought she'd moved on after Rider walked away. Until her dog is brutally killed and threatening letters start arriving, giving her no choice but to trust the man who broke her heart. She just wishes her brother Jason, who welcomes his former best friend back with open arms, wouldn't ask uncomfortable questions about the past that Rider isn't ready to answer.

As the investigation intensifies, clues surface, pointing to a sinister threat lurking closer than they imagined. With a killer watching their every move and their past feelings complicating everything, Rider and Junelle must confront both their painful past and a deadly present before they become the next victims.

Perfect for fans of high-stakes thrillers who crave their love stories with a dangerous edge. One-click ***Fatal Consequences*** *now and discover how far one detective will go to protect the woman he never stopped loving.*

ABOUT THE AUTHOR

I'm a *USA Today* Bestselling Author that loves to write contemporary romance and romantic suspense novels, although I am partial to romantic suspense. I even dabble in paranormal. Honestly, I love anything that has to do with romance. As long as there's a happy ending, I'm a happy camper. And insta-love...yes, please! I love baseball (Go Twins!) and creating awesome crafts. I graduated with a Bachelor's Degree in Criminal Justice, working in that field for several years before I became a stay-at-home mom. I have a few more amazing stories in the works. If you would like to learn more about me and my books, head to my website by scanning the QR code. Thanks for reading!

www.ingramcontent.com/pod-product-compliance
Lightning Source LLC
LaVergne TN
LVHW091049080826
845145LV00002B/677

* 9 7 8 1 9 5 5 8 8 6 6 8 0 *